A Soldier's

Last Mission

A sequel to
The Last Yard Sale

by
Marie LeClaire

D1275798

Published by
Create Space
ISBN-13: 978-1722913014
ISBN-10: 1722913010
Barnes and Noble
ISBN-13: 9781722913014

Cover Art by https://www.selfpubbookcovers.com/RLSather

"Fiction is the lie through which we tell the truth."

- Albert Camus

Chapter 1

It was a beautiful Saturday afternoon in October and Marybeth was on her way home from a full day of yard saleing as usual. Her shop, One Woman's Junque: An Antique Boutique, featured recreated and re-purposed items she collected each week from around the greater Pomroy area. She gained some notoriety when her shop appeared in the blogs of the few travelers who ventured into the small town an hour and a half outside of Philadelphia. They came out to escape the busy city life and spend a few days in quieter surroundings. Her store offered a nice alternative to the local antique markets, and people appreciated her creative use of cast-off items. Usually, she used the drive home to begin the mental process of re-birthing the day's purchases into their next life. Today, however, she was a little preoccupied.

Josh was arriving in town on Tuesday. She hated to admit how much she looked forward to his visits. She was still guarded about relationships in general, and worried that she was just setting herself up for disappointment. How long had they been doing the long-distance romance now? It was hard to believe it had been almost a year. So far so good, but it took her marriage a couple of years before it started going sideways. So, time wasn't telling anything yet.

As she mentally chronicled the past few months, events from last Fall flooded into her mind. Had they been perched on the edge of her awareness waiting for a chance to charge in? The onslaught didn't surprise her. Initially, it had required a fair amount of mental energy to keep them at bay. It got easier as time passed. Now she wasn't sure how much she could even believe.

It all began with a strange yard sale and four peculiar items. There was the doll that had helped to reconnect her with her sister, Regina. The music box that had played the song from her wedding, pushing her to get honest about her marriage and divorce. The family photograph took her down the road of her own family history. And lastly, the book, with its message for Josh on the inside cover. And that wasn't even the bizarre part.

Allowing herself this momentary peek into the past, she realized that the whole series of events had begun right around this time last year. Yes, it was a beautiful Fall day just like today. She had been on her way home from yard saleing when she had spotted one more sign that she just couldn't pass up. In fact, it might have been this exact weekend. Was it? How odd that she would be remembering things on just this day.

It had all started with a yard sale hosted by Josh's mother from beyond the grave. The recollection made her shudder. Did it really happen that way? Time gave her the luxury of rationalizing the events as vivid dreams or an overactive imagination. But her relationship with Josh had come out of that moment and there certainly was no dismissing *that* as imagination. Was there?

Marybeth shook her head, forcing the memories back from whence they came.

"Focus on your driving before you kill someone," she admonished herself out loud, shifting her attention to the road. "How do I get home from here?"

She began to mentally plot her drive back to the house from her current location.

"Let's see, I think this will take me back to Bramble Road then to Rt. 10, then to Main Street." She pulled out onto the deserted country road, heading back toward Pomroy. That's when she saw it, on an empty stretch of road just like before. The Yard Sale sign. It wasn't *any* yard sale sign. It was *the* Yard Sale sign. Old wood with hand-painted letters. The same sign she had spotted a year ago under just these circumstances. Her heart rate quickened. She felt a knot forming in her gut.

She instantly decided to pass it by. After all, if she'd learned anything from last year it was that she didn't have to stop at every sign she saw. Especially this one. Life had settled down nicely and she wasn't about to go looking for trouble. She drove past the sign.

"See," she said to the air, "I don't have to stop and I'm not going to."

Just as she was feeling empowered, she saw the same sign at the next side street.

"I will not turn. I will not turn," she told herself, fighting off the urge to do just that. "Let someone else stop."

She drove past the second sign. As she rounded the next twist in the road, there it was again, at the end of a rural country lane.

3

"Damn!" she shouted as she banged on the steering wheel. She pulled over onto the shoulder. Staring at the sign in front of her, she felt anger rising up her spine.

"Why me!" she demanded. "I won't!" she yelled at the sign. It seemed to stare back at her mockingly.

She thought about the old woman. Then about Josh. Truth was, her life had gotten significantly better since that yard sale a year ago and so had the lives of others. But things had settled down to a predictable routine and she wanted to keep it that way.

"Fine," she said with resignation as she turned down the small road. It curved around, over a brook and past a couple of houses set back from the shoulder, but no yard sale materialized. She was thinking that she might be off the hook when a small farmhouse appeared at the end of the road. The kind with the wraparound porch and window shutters. On the lawn a few feet away from the porch's edge sat a table. She pulled up in front, got out and looked around for the old woman, but she was nowhere in sight. She was about to make a quick get-away when a young man appeared on the front porch. He stood very still, looking at her, hands in his pockets. He was wearing a green army tee shirt with dog tags hanging low around his neck. Green army pants were tucked into black boots. He looked to be about twenty and had a slightly timid demeanor.

"Good afternoon, Ma'am," he greeted her.

"Good afternoon," Marybeth replied. "I was expecting an old woman."

"Yes, Ma'am. Are you Marybeth? She told me you'd come by."

"Oh, she did, did she?" She looked up into the sky. "And it's MB now, thank you," she corrected, annoyance clear in her

4

voice. She turned back to the soldier. "What? Do I have some kind of reputation in the afterlife now?"

"I can't say, Ma-am. She just said that you'd be able to help."

Marybeth let out a huff. "Very well, then." She resigned herself to the situation and her attitude turned a bit kinder. "What do you think I can do for you?"

"Well, Ma-am, I have a couple of things that I need to get rid of." He walked to the spindly railing at the edge of the porch and nodded his head toward the table. Marybeth turned to look. On the table sat two items, an army helmet and a stack of papers tied together with string. They were sitting close to each other as if they belonged together.

"These are yours then?" she asked, turning back to the young man.

"Yes, ma-am. I don't recall much except that I have these things that I don't need anymore." He pulled a hand from his pocket and gestured to the table with a slight shrug of his shoulders.

Marybeth walked slowly over to the table. Her insides were considering the options, to run like hell or stay the course. When she got to the table, she looked up at the man who had asked for her assistance. He seemed almost childlike, barely a man, really. Too young, she thought, to be dead.

"Is it okay if I pick them up?" She knew it would be the point of no return.

"Yes, ma-am."

She reached down to pick up the helmet and braced herself for what she suspected was coming. And she was right.

* * *

Suddenly, reality turned fuzzy and she found herself in what appeared to be an army compound. A

5

truck with a canvas cover and open back was heading out of the yard carrying twenty or so soldiers. The young man from the porch was hanging off the open end, reaching out for a helmet offered by a soldier on the ground just out of Marybeth's sight.

"Thanks, man," the young soldier yelled from the retreating truck. "I'll get it back to you. I swear. In the meantime, mine's in the mess hall. You're welcome to it."

"No problem," a voice called back.

"Hey, it was good talking to you."

"Likewise," replied the voice. "Keep your head low."

"Low as I can go." And with a mock salute, he passed through the razor wire fence and around the bend.

Marybeth could see the shadow of the man standing near her as he watched the truck drive out of sight. She couldn't be sure, but he seemed oddly familiar.

* * *

Then she was back on the lawn, reaching for the table to steady herself.

The young man spoke. "You know how sometimes the briefest of conversations can make the biggest difference?" the soldier was asking.

"Yes. I do." Marybeth thought for a moment of the woman's shelter she donated to and how sometimes even the shortest of conversations can be uplifting to another human being.

The soldier continued, "That man eased my burden just a bit that day and I never got a chance to thank him."

"Is that it, then?" she asked, sounding a bit put-out. "Is all this about an overdue thank you?"

"No, ma-am. I think that man can save my son's life."

She immediately felt bad about her attitude. "Okay," she softened. "What can I do?"

"All you need to do is give him that helmet."

"Okay. Who is he?" She was thinking this was sounding easy.

"I don't know. I just met him that day. I can't seem to recall his name.

"Great." Marybeth asked a bit incredulously. She stared at the young soldier waiting for more information.

"The old woman said you'd know."

"Oh, she did?"

"Yes, ma'am."

Not hiding her irritation, she placed the helmet on the table and turned her attention to the papers. "What's this?"

It appeared to be a leather journal and a pile of letters tied together with twine. Before she could think twice, she was picking it up.

* * *

Marybeth found herself in a large crowd of people, some crying, some hugging, some in army dress uniforms. She spotted her soldier standing with a young woman. Cradled between them was an infant wearing a blue bonnet. They were holding each other tight. The woman was crying.

"I love you Becky, with every breath I take, until the day I die, and then maybe some more after that. But if I don't come back, James needs a father, so you find him a good one. Promise me."

"I won't have any of this talk, Bobby. You're coming back. I just know it."

"No, you don't know it. So, promise me. Promise me James will have a good father."

"I won't."

"Promise!"

"I can't," she broke down into sobs. *"I can't even think of it. I love you too much."*

"Promise me before I go, Becky. Please," he was almost begging her.

"Okay. I promise! But I know I won't need to because you'll be coming back." Becky was regaining some of her composure now.

A loud horn sounded.

"That's it then. I have to go. I love you."

"I love you back. Be careful."

Marybeth watched as the soldier headed for the bus that would take him and the others off to war.

* * *

Then she was back on the lawn in the setting sun. Her eyes were moist with tears as she contemplated the items on the table. She turned to address the soldier, but he was gone.

"Great." She looked around. No soldier, no neighbors, no other cars. Just silence. She collected the items and headed to her car.

"Here we go again."

Chapter 2

Marybeth was making her way back home, just as she had on that fateful day one year ago. And just like a year ago, she was arguing with herself about accepting magical items from ghostly sellers.

"What in the world made me take on something like this again?" she demanded of herself out loud. "Is this another breakdown?" She looked in the rear-view mirror for the items. Sure enough, there they were. "How am I supposed to know what to do with a helmet and a bunch of letters?"

"*The old woman said you'd know.*" Marybeth mockingly repeated the young man's words. "Oh, she did, did she?"

Marybeth continued the argument with herself as she wound her way back home, knowing full well that she was now committed to seeing this through. Even as she resisted, she went into problem-solving mode. Where would she start? The only person she could think of to talk to was her dad. He served in the Army in Vietnam. Was her young soldier a Vietnam vet too? His uniform wasn't the standard desert camouflage that she saw soldiers wearing today. It had more of the M*A*S*H look to it.

Her dad had been tasked with processing the bodies of fallen soldiers before they were loaded on a plane for home. When they had talked about it briefly last year, it had caused a flair up of old PTSD stuff causing him to return to the VA for therapy. She still felt bad about it. Did she want to risk her father's health to help the already dead? Why wasn't anything ever simple?

As she approached her house, she got the next surprise of the day. Josh's car in the driveway. She hated surprises. What was he doing here? He was two days early. Shit. The house was a mess and she hadn't been shopping in more than a week. Why hadn't he called? Was something wrong? She was trying to decide between irritation and concern as she backed up to the garage door and parked.

She sat in the car for a moment deciding what to do next. Usually she emptied out her purchases as soon as she got home so she could relax for the evening. Her eyes glanced back at the last two items of the day, then to Josh's car. Unloading would have to wait as irritation was taking over. She headed in through the kitchen door to see Josh smiling at her from the kitchen table and drinking a cup of coffee.

"What are you doing here?" she asked.

He noticed the irritation immediately. It set off triggers from his own past. His relationship with Jan had started going south with just this tone. He tried the calming approach. "Didn't you get my text?" he replied.

"No. You know I don't like surprises."

"I understand. It's not a surprise. I texted you that I was coming. Twice."

"It only counts if I read it," she retorted.

"I have no control over that," Josh bristled back. "Is there some reason I shouldn't be here?" His voice has the slight inclination of an accusation.

"No." She backed off a bit and shifted gears. "I've been busy. That's all. The house is a mess. I have no food and I haven't looked at my phone all day."

"I knew you would be yard saleing, so I texted you this morning that I was coming down early. I just got here. There's a fresh pot of coffee on." He knew by now that the warm brown elixir could ease most situations. As expected, she put down her keys and poured herself a cup.

"I'm sorry. It's good to see you. I've had a weird day is all. And this just threw off me a little bit more." She was still a little edgy.

"Look, if this is a problem, I can leave."

"No. No. Just give me a minute." She paced the kitchen a bit.

"What's got you so jacked up?" He was getting a little concerned.

There was a long pause. She hadn't expected to see anyone, and she was still sorting out the day's events for herself. She wasn't ready to talk about it.

"First, tell me what you're doing here," she deflected.

"You're not going to like it."

She rolled her eyes and looked to the heavens. "What's wrong?"

"I had a dream last night. About my mother."

At first, he assumed the appearance of his mother was just a memory that snuck into his dream state. But it was so vivid, and she had been so insistent, he knew something was up.

She took a deep breath and sighed irritably.

"You don't look surprised," Josh observed.

"No," was all she could say.

"Why not?"

"You first," she said, as she sat down across from him with a mug that said *Give me coffee and no one gets hurt.*

Josh hesitated now, wondering how to proceed, seeing that Marybeth was already out of sorts. He opted to ease in.

"So, I had a dream last night. It was a little weird. Okay, maybe a lot. I don't know yet."

"Just get to the point, please."

"Okay, okay. So much for setup. I saw my mom. She was dressed in some kind of army green clothing. She had a helmet and she kept waving it around insisting that I make sure he gets it. 'Help Marybeth. He has to get it,' she kept saying. She was very insistent, almost stern, you know, in that motherly way. She hesitated a minute, listening to something I couldn't hear, then said 'Go now!' Then I woke up."

Marybeth sat quietly for a moment, taking this in with a scowl on her face.

"I was going to do it," she said into the air.

"Do what?" came the calm query from Josh.

Marybeth sighed. "I stopped at a yard sale today."

"Yes, that's what you usually do on Saturdays."

"It was the last stop of the day."

"Yes?" Josh prompted cautiously. This was starting to sound familiar. "And who was having the sale?"

"Not your mother, if that's what you're asking?"

"Okay." Again, it was a cautious reply.

"But it had that same flavor, if you know what I mean. Apparently, your mother was behind it."

"Okay." Josh was getting frustrated. "It's your turn. Why don't you just tell me what happened."

Marybeth took a long pull on her coffee as if it were whiskey, then stared out the window before she started talking. "I was on my way home today, on one of those back roads south of town, when I realized that today was the day that I happened onto that strange yard sale last year that proved to be orchestrated by your mother."

Josh nodded. Unlike Marybeth, he had played the events of last year over and over, marveling at his mother's involvement. His mother's death had set off the cascade of events that had brought them together.

Marybeth continued. "I was trying my best to shake it out of my head when I saw the sign. *Yard Sale*." She waved her hand in the air horizontally, indicating an imaginary sign. "It was the same sign I saw a year ago. Exactly the same. I got a little freaked out and tried to dodge it. I drove past it, thinking that I wasn't going to do this again. But then the sign appeared at the next road and then the next." Marybeth's voice had become pleading, as if she needed Josh to understand that she had no choice but to stop.

"I get it," Josh reassured her. "My mother was nothing if not persistent." He flashed her an apologetic smile.

Her tension eased slightly as she told him the rest of the story, including being irritated at seeing his car in the driveway. "I don't know what to do now."

Josh's first thought was Marybeth's father. "Are you going to call Sean? He's the only veteran I know."

"I don't know yet. You know what happened last time I talked to him about Vietnam."

"I know. Where are the items now?"

"In the back of my car with the rest of the stuff from today."

"Okay, here's my suggestion. Let's leave everything there and go get dinner. My guess is that you haven't eaten all day."

"What's your point?" she said flatly, with a slight bit of accusation.

"No point really." He tried to lighten the moment. "It's not like I'm saying that you get confused and irritated when your blood sugar goes down, and you don't think clearly and maybe get a little bitchy. I'm not saying that at all."

"Alright," she yielded. She knew he was right. "Let's go get dinner."

They both got up at the same time and stood looking at each other for a moment then laughed. Opening their arms, they reached out for the embrace that had gotten overlooked when she first arrived. They stood holding each other for a long moment, physically reconnecting after four weeks apart.

"I'm glad you're here." she said.

"Me too."

They had both come to enjoy this moment which usually lead to the shedding of cloths and great sex. But the events of the day and lack of food proved to be the driving force at the moment. Josh was the first to step back.

"Okay, food first."

"Yes. I'm afraid so," she agreed.

They were laughing as they headed out the door.

Chapter 3

April 3, 1970

Private First Class Sean Morgan was sitting by himself in the busy mess hall, having lunch alone as usual. Most of the guys kept their distance from him. His job, processing bodies as they came in from various combat zones, gave people the willies. Some thought he was jinxed or cursed. Others complained that he smelled like death. He understood, sort of. He had been "weirded" out by his job at first too. Now the constant sideways looks were old. It was hard enough being in Vietnam without this. The isolation was wearing away at his spirit. He toughed it out the best he could with memories of home and the promise of the American Dream that awaited him upon his return, now just 98 days away. Today he was surprised to see a soldier headed his way with his lunch tray.

"Mind if I sit down?" he asked politely.

"Not at all. I'd be grateful for the company."

"My name's Bobby."

"Hey Bobby. I'm Sean."

They shook hands over the table.

"How come you're all by yourself over here in the corner?" Bobby asked.

"I give people the creeps, I guess."

"Really, how come?"

Sean wasn't sure he wanted to talk about it, fearing that this guy, too, would run for the hills.

"I process the dead all day. Some of the guys call me the Grim Reaper. They say I smell like death."

"Well, Sean, I'm not particularly creeped out by your job, but I can't deny there is a bit of a smell coming off you."

"Yeah. I know. I can't get it out of my clothes."

"Tough break. I saw you out there this morning, with the bodies."

Bobby had watched Sean earlier in the day, out in the compound, after a helicopter had unloaded a dozen or so bodies. He was struck by the care that Sean seemed to take with each one. Sean would kneel down on one knee with his clip board, completing the paperwork, making sure numbers matched with dog tags, but it seemed like there was more to it than that. He could see Sean talking to them. Not gabbing it up or obviously thinking out loud. Sean would pause with his head tilted slightly sideways, appear to say something under his breath and then listen. After a moment or two he would write something down on the clipboard, nod his head almost imperceptibly and move on to the next body bag.

"I've seen a lot of them go down in the field," Bobby said, lowering his eyes and pushing his food around the plate. Sean knew that Bobby was with an infantry unit that had just come in from the fighting.

"That's got to be worse," Sean said.

"No worse, no better, I imagine," Bobby replied. He hesitated before asking, "Anything weird ever happen to you when you're with them?" Bobby nodded out towards the now empty compound.

Sean paused. No one ever asked him about his job.

"Weird how?" he asked cautiously.

"Like, did you ever think you saw something unusual?" Bobby asked slowly.

The question was intense and sincere, spoken in a low voice, as if Bobby had something more to say.

"Yeah, sometimes," Sean admitted. "How 'bout you?"

"Sometimes I think I see their spirits, Sean. I know that sounds crazy and maybe it is, but I swear I see this mist hovering over their bodies like it's their soul or something."

It was Sean's turn to push his food around. "Why are you telling me this?"

Bobby looked out to the courtyard. "When I saw you out there, when you were finishing up on the paperwork, I could see that vapor drift up to heaven, one by one, when you were done with them."

They both sat quietly for a moment, neither one looking at the other.

Sean broke the silence. "Sometimes I think I hear them talking to me."

"When you're down on one knee like that?"

"Yeah. At the bottom of the form there's a place for comments, last words or circumstances. At some point I started wondering what they might want their family to know, what I'd want my family to know if it were me going home in a bag. So, one day I asked one, ya' know, not expecting any answer of course, just thinking out loud. Next thing I know,

17

I'm hearing this voice in my head saying, "Tell my mom to be proud of me."

Sean looked up, waiting to see what kind of a response he was getting. Bobby sat quiet, spellbound.

"I know it sounds freaky, but I'm not crazy, Bobby. At least I don't think so."

"I don't think you are either, Sean. No crazier than the rest of us, anyway. Then what happened?"

"I started asking every body that came through the camp and each time there was some message that came to me to pass on. It's been happening ever since. Truly, it's the only thing that keeps me from losing my mind. Sometimes I think I'm just making it up, you know, some psychological coping skill or something."

"I know what you mean. The first time I saw the vapor out in the field, I thought I was losing it. But then it kept happening. Now, I can tell if I should go after a downed soldier or not. If I don't see the vapor, I know he's still alive and I need to do whatever I can to get him safe. If I see the vapor, I know it can wait till the fighting stops. I've never said anything to anyone 'til now, 'til after I saw you out in the yard today."

They were both sitting there, silently, taking in the other one's story when the sergeant came by bellowing, "Are you guys gonna sit around here all damn day? We got a war to fight. Remember?"

Sean and Bobby jumped up with their trays and moved out before the sergeant could find some extra work for them, like kitchen duty. They headed off to their respective units, but not before a handshake and a promise to continue the conversation later.

Chapter 4

Marybeth and Josh caught up on things over dinner, not that there was a lot to catch up on. They talked nearly every day and had gotten together many times over the year, either in Pomroy or Connecticut or somewhere in between. The long-distance romance was difficult at times, but they seemed to weather the storms, always with positive gains. Neither one was looking for anything more than the status quo, or at least neither one brought it up. They were half way through dinner when Josh finally brought up the question that was screaming to be asked.

"What are you going to do now?"

"I have no idea. Ask your mother," she said with an overlay of sarcasm.

"Look, this isn't my fault, just for the record."

"Yeah, sorry."

"Do you want to do a little brain storming or should I just leave it alone?" he offered.

"I don't know. You have any ideas?" They both paused a moment to think.

Josh started it off with, "The only veteran that I know is Sean."

"I know," whined Marybeth with a grimace. "I really don't want to bring him into this. I still feel bad about last year."

"Your father doesn't hold you in any way responsible for that, and he's feeling fine now. Probably better than you. In fact, he reconnected with a few old friends and has made the whole experience into some kind of grass roots thing, hasn't he?"

Josh was right. Dad had taken a problem and made it into a social group and now a community resource for the newest wave of veterans discharging from active service. Still, she was reluctant to bring him into this. Especially since she hadn't told him anything about the first yard sale.

"What am I supposed to tell him. 'I have these magical items and I don't know what to do with them? Do you?'"

"Well, no. But maybe we can at least get some information about the young man. Maybe he has access to old records, next of kin, things like that."

"True. He could at least be a resource."

"Sure. It's the only thing I can think of at this moment. Maybe when we look over the items something else will come to us."

"Like another vision or something?" Marybeth was getting a little worked up again.

"That, or just another idea," he said, trying to reassure her.

"Okay. Let's do that." Marybeth said, getting up from the table.

Josh paid the check and followed her out.

On the way home, they worked out the logistics for the next few days. Because Josh had arrived early, there were chores still to do and she still hadn't unloaded the car. Then there was laundry, grocery shopping and a little bit of yard work. The leaves had started to fall and the lawn needed mowing. All things she planned to do before Josh's arrival on Tuesday. And, of course, there was her shop. Angie would be there tomorrow and Monday to help with the latest purchases, but Marybeth had to be there to make final decisions about inventory and pricing. She wondered for a moment what Angie would have to say about the helmet and letters. Maybe she shouldn't tell her. Angie was a force to be reckoned with when there was a cause. She decided to decide later as they pulled into the driveway.

They unloaded Marybeth's yard sale purchases into the garage, then took the last two items into the house. Placing the items on the coffee table, they seated themselves on the couch.

"Tell me again what the young man said about the helmet," Josh asked as he turned the helmet over in his hands.

"He said I needed to 'give him that helmet' and that he can 'save my son's life.'"

"No other identifier?"

"No!" Marybeth with irritation.

"Okay, okay, sorry. Let's shift gears and look at the letters."

"Are you sure? That feels like such a huge invasion of privacy."

"MB, he's dead. Moreover, he left us these things to help save his son from something. I think we can read them."

"Right. Of course."

Marybeth untied the twine holding the bundle together and put the journal to the side. When she separated the letters, a silver necklace spilled out onto the coffee table. It was a small silver medallion, about the size of a quarter, on a black silk cord. A round pale green stone sat in the center of a simple geometric design cut into the silver.

"Whoa! What's this?" Marybeth stared at the jewelry on the table, hesitant to touch it.

When Josh reached over and picked it up, Marybeth caught her breath. Josh looked over at her.

"It's okay. Look. No visions." He waved his hands in front of him, the necklace draped around one finger.

Marybeth exhaled. "Well, be careful," she admonished. "You never know."

"Even if there were, we already know, they're harmless."

"Until someone pokes an eye out," she mumbled under her breath.

Josh was inspecting the medallion. "It's simple enough, no inscription or anything. It looks like the stone is peridot."

"How do you even know that?"

"An article I wrote for National Geographic about labor abuse at the mines in Brazil."

Marybeth shook her head. "Okay, a peridot medallion. What's it doing in here? Was it a present for his wife that he never gave her? It's too feminine to be his."

"That's a good guess, but what would he be doing with it in Vietnam?"

Marybeth retrieved the piece from Josh, looked at it closely for a moment. "Who knows. It's one more mystery to be solved I guess." She placed it on the table and sifted through the letters for any more unexpected items. Not finding any she started gently unfolding each sheet, fearing it would crumble in her hands. The paper seemed to have held up well over the years. She wondered if heaven had acid free storage boxes in climate-controlled rooms.

A Soldier's Last Mission

Each correspondence was from Becky to Bobby and were already placed in chronological order. She picked up the first note and started reading aloud. They were love letters of course. Not much information about people or places that might lend some sort of clue.

As Marybeth read aloud, Josh jotted down notes. The letters validated Marybeth's vision of Bobby and Becky with their son, James. But last names were absent and the envelopes for the letters were missing. It turns out the young soldier was in fact from the Vietnam War. 1970 to be exact. His wife and son were apparently living on a base somewhere in the states while he was overseas. Although all this was mildly interesting, the information seemed useless forty years later.

They reversed the process for the journal, with Josh reading and Marybeth taking notes. They were both quickly absorbed into the recounting of the day to day business of war. Unfortunately, it, too, was missing the kind of details they were looking for, and, thankfully, it lacked any of the gore.

"Let me see the helmet again," Josh asked Marybeth.

She handed it to him. "I don't see what you'll get from that except maybe his hat size."

"I don't know either," he said, inspecting the helmet more closely. "I see things too, you know," he kidded.

"You do not. I see things. You just see pretty colors," she jested back. She was referring to auric fields of energy around people and objects that Josh could sometimes see. "So? You got anything?" she prodded.

"Not any pretty colors, but there's something written in here." He was holding it under the light from the living room lamp. "It's a number of some kind. Hand written. Do you think it identifies the owner, like a serial number?"

"I don't know. Maybe. That's something I can ask my dad. I'll call him in the morning." She took a deep breath and put her notebook and pen on the table. "Right now, I'd like to put this stuff away and spend the rest of the evening doing something besides talking." She looked at him with eyebrows raised as she removed the helmet from his hands.

"Oh yeah?" he asked.

"Oh. Yeah." she smiled.

Chapter 5

Marybeth was having her first cup of coffee by 6 AM. She had woken up early and immediately started worrying about calling her dad. Early morning worrying was something she used to do when she was with Eric, when there was plenty to worry about. So now, besides concern for her dad, she was wondering if she was backsliding in some way into the darkness that had ended her marriage. Well, she assured herself, she could worry about that later and she probably would, but right now she needed a strategy to approach her dad about the war.

What was she going to say? How much information should she tell him? The strange visions from last year had prompted a conversation with her dad about his past. She hadn't asked any big questions, or so she thought. *How did you meet mom?* didn't seem like a life altering question at the time, but it had indeed pried opened Pandora's box. That's when she found out he had been diagnosed with Post Traumatic Stress Disorder, PTSD for short, and that thinking back to those times had "chased some memories out of the corners and into the light" as he put it. She wasn't sure she wanted to risk it again. On the other hand, as Josh had pointed out, something good had come out of it. Her dad had met up with some old friends at the VA and they had started a small unofficial group that supported the new batch of injured warriors from Iraq and Afghanistan.

She paced the kitchen with her coffee and her thoughts, getting more agitated with each pass. She needed to talk this out with Josh. He was sleeping in, as usual. She looked at the clock. It was 6:15 Sunday morning. Okay, maybe not sleeping in exactly. Nonetheless, she needed to talk to him. Meanwhile, he was catching the z's that had eluded her.

The questions looped back around again. When should she call her dad? He was an early riser too, but he usually went to mass at 9:30. She didn't want to alarm him before church, so that meant that she had to wait until at least 11:00. Or if she called him before church, he had some time to process the conversation and maybe get a little Godly guidance or something. She was back and forth with each pass across the kitchen. Just when she was starting to climb the walls, a sleepy-eyed Josh shuffled into the kitchen.

"What in God's name are you doing up at this hour on a Sunday morning...when you could be lying in bed with me?"

"Well, you weren't much company when I got up," she said dryly.

"Could be true, especially if you were looking for an argument," he replied to her tone.

"Sorry. I'm already twisted up about talking to my dad. I wish there were some other way to figure this out," she said pacing the floor.

He came up to her, hooked his arm around her waist and pulled her close. "Why don't you come back to bed and we can talk about it," he said while kissing her neck.

"Mmmmmmmm. Nice offer but..."

"But you can't get your mind off this other stuff, can you?" he interrupted her.

"No. Sorry."

"Okay, where's breakfast?"

"On the counter, next to the coffee." They had thought to get something for breakfast last night on the way home. The Donut Hole hadn't had much left, but it would at least get them through till the diner opened at 8:00. Josh poured himself a cup of coffee, grabbed a honey glazed eye-opener and settled himself in at the table.

"Okay, what's got you pacing?"

"I'm worried about my dad!" she snapped, as if it should be obvious.

"Look, I'm not really awake yet so if you want to have this conversation with me, you need to be nicer."

"I'm sorry," she said again. That was her third apology so far this morning and Josh had only been up for 5 minutes. Snapping at every little thing was also an old pattern, looking externally for the cause of her discontent. She was working hard to steer clear of past mistakes. She needed to regroup.

"I'll be right back." Spinning around on her heels, she marched herself into the living room, took a deep breath, physically shook her body to loosen the tension, and headed back into the kitchen. "Okay, can I get a do-over?"

"Yes, please," Josh replied.

"Good morning, honey. How did you sleep?" she asked politely.

Josh opened his mouth to reply, but before he could get a word out, she was moving on. "Never mind that. I'm really worried about dad and I have been waiting for you to get up so

I can talk about it with you. I didn't want to wake you up, but then I got mad that you were sleeping."

"You know that's a little crazy right?"

"Being worried about my dad or being mad at you for sleeping?"

"Well, both."

"This whole situation is a little crazy. Here I am, once again, with crazy items and a crazy task from a crazy woman."

"Hey, easy on my mom," Josh kidded, trying to break the mood. "And, really, she wasn't even there."

"A technicality," Marybeth said with a wave of her hand. She was starting to lighten up. "I guess I'm mad at myself too, for walking back into this... this... whatever this is." The first bizarre yard sale had pushed her to her limit. She continued to pace.

After a moment of silence, Josh asked, "What did you do with those cards that belonged to my mother?" He was referring to a deck of tarot cards his mother had used for most of her life.

"They're in the desk drawer. Why?"

"Just wondering. If she's in the background here, maybe she has something to say.

"Fine, but neither of us know how to use them."

"I don't think we have to do the whole setup. Just pick a card or two and see what they say."

"I don't know." Marybeth was skeptical even though her own experiences had shown her there were things that just couldn't be explained.

"Look, it can't hurt, it might help," Josh offered as he headed for the desk drawer.

"Sure. I guess so."

Josh returned from the living room with a small bundle wrapped in a colorful cloth. He put it on the table and sat down. Marybeth took the chair opposite him.

"Okay, they're your mother's cards. You must have seen her use them. Did she ever do a reading for you?"

"Yeah, but I never really paid much attention. Mostly what I know is that the person asking the question has to shuffle the cards for a long time, 2 minutes maybe, while they think about their question."

"Okay." Marybeth unwrapped the cards and laid out the cloth. Then she handed the cards to Josh.

"Oh, noooooo," he waved his hands in front of the cards. "It's your helmet, it's your question."

"You're a coward and a hypocrite," she said, sounding appalled, and trying not to laugh.

"I thought that's what you loved about me?" he replied with that grin that melted Marybeth's heart every time.

"Fine. I'll do it. Here, you look them up." She pushed the book at him. "So, what do I do?"

"Think about what you want to ask, like 'Is my father the one to help with this task?' or 'Will I hurt my father by asking him about this?' or anything else you want to know about or any other way you want to ask the question."

"Okay. Will my father be okay if I involve him in all this drama?" She looked down at the deck of cards in her hands. She noticed that she was trembling slightly. She began to gently shuffle the cards. She and Josh sat in silence. After about two minutes, the energy in the room had changed for Marybeth. She could feel electricity in the air and a sense of calm had come over her. She straightened the deck and set it on the cloth. "Now what?" she asked quietly.

"My mom would turn over the top card." he said.

She flipped the top card, placed it beside the deck and read it out loud. "Judgment. Number 20. Oh, that sounds bad."

"No, no. Mom always said there are no bad cards. We just have to read about it." Josh opened the book and found the page for Judgment. He read aloud:

> The Judgment card calls for a period of reflection and self-evaluation.

"See, that doesn't sound bad." he reassured her. She looked at him skeptically. He continued reading aloud.

> Judgment tells you that you are close to reaching a significant stage in your own journey. The Judgment card suggests that you have reviewed and evaluated your past experiences and have learned from them. All the pieces of the puzzle of your life are finally coming together to form one, integrated picture of your life story. This integration has healed any deep wounds and you are now in a position to put the past behind you. Now, you are ready to confront any unfinished business.
>
> Judgment is about finding absolution and releasing guilt and sorrow about the past. As with everything in life, the beginning is woven irrevocably into the end and the end will eventually lead to a new beginning. Put the past behind you and look to the future, ready to begin again.

"There. That doesn't seem bad at all. In fact, it seems kind of uplifting," he said, trying to convince her.

"Do you think my dad has some unresolved issues from the past?"

"I think anyone who goes to war probably has a lifetime of unresolved issues about it. I haven't been to war, so I don't pretend to know. But everyone plays the 'Wish I had' or 'Wish I hadn't' game at some point in their lives, and I guess the game is a bit bigger when you have that kind of experience."

"Okay, I guess. Maybe not so bad after all. But it still sounds like it could kick up his PTSD stuff."

"Or resolve it." Josh offered the other side of the coin. "Maybe you could start by asking your dad if it's okay to talk about it. Let him decide."

"Of course!" she almost yelled at this new possibility. "Great idea. That way he can say no if he wants to." Marybeth immediately relaxed as this new option settled into her brain. "Okay, that was easy. Well, actually, it wasn't that easy. I'm really glad you're here. I probably would have stewed about it for another few hours." She continued to unwind, physically feeling the tension draining from her body.

"Things will be clearer when we talk to your dad."

"Yes, but I can't do that for another few hours and you know patience isn't my best thing."

"Alright, here's a plan. We have about an hour before the diner opens for breakfast. Let's get dressed and take another look at what we have. After breakfast, we call your dad and give him a heads up. Then hit the internet and see what information we can get from there, even if it's just historical. I don't know anything about that era, do you?"

"Another great idea. And no, just what my dad told me last year which wasn't much." Marybeth was feeling much better now that she had a game plan to work with.

"So, we're good?"

"Yeah." Marybeth finally exhaled.

"Good, because I want to talk to you about something."

"Oooohhhh. That doesn't sound good."

"It's fine. Really. It's just that we don't talk about us very much and, well, it's our anniversary. Or maybe you hadn't noticed."

"I noticed." Marybeth was on the defensive. She avoided any conversation about their relationship or where it might be going.

"We can argue the official date, but mostly I'm using the Jack-O-Lantern Festival as a general marker." They had met a few weeks before the festival and their first date had been carving pumpkins for the shelving in front of her store.

"What's your point?"

"I thought it would be nice if we did something special, you know, to celebrate." Josh was somewhere between cautious and nonchalant.

"You know I'm still taking this one day at a time, right?"

"I know. Still, one year is an accomplishment for both of us. Worth at least a nice dinner, don't you think?"

"Okay, sure." She softened some. "What did you have in mind?"

"Pumpkin carving on Friday, followed by dinner. This time at the Crabby Apple."

"Ah. A step up from last year." She smiled at the memory. Last year's carving had been followed by soup and snacks at the bed and breakfast in town.

"I thought it was warranted."

"So it is. You'll make it happen?"

"I will."

Chapter 6

Marybeth and Josh strategized about the phone call to her dad on the way to breakfast. Although she had had some heartfelt conversations with him a year ago, she had never said anything about the strange yard sale or visions that she and others had experienced. She was sure her sister, Regina, hadn't either. In fact, even she and Regina hadn't talked about it much since it all happened. That part of her family tradition, not talking about things, hadn't changed much.

No matter how much she planned, she knew that once her father picked up the phone, all bets would be off as to what came out of her mouth. What if he offers to help? What if he has a vision and thinks he's crazy? What if it all pushes him too far over the edge? What if...What if...What if..... Now she was just making *herself* crazy. She was going to have to play it by ear and be as cautious as she could.

She was getting ready to dial the phone when it rang. It was her dad. She let out a yelp and dropped the phone, then scrambled to pick it back up.

"What's the matter?" Josh asked shifting his focus from driving to Marybeth.

"It's my dad." She was almost stuttering.

"Well, answer it!"

"Hello Dad?" Her heart was pounding, and her voice was shaky.

"Yeah, honey. Are you okay? Is something wrong?"

"No (she lied), uh, I was just going to call you. That's all. Ah...how's it going?"

Sean knew his daughter better than that. "It's going fine, Marybeth. What's on your mind?" He was not fond of Marybeth's name change and preferred to stay with the name he had given her at the start.

She took a deep breath and launched into her rehearsed spiel. "I picked up a couple of military items at a yard sale yesterday and I was wondering if you might tell me a little about them, but I don't want it to cause you any stress or, you know, anything else. So only if it feels okay."

"I appreciate your concern. Let me know what you have, and I'll tell you if I can help out."

"Well, I have this helmet. I'm not sure how old it is and it has some sort of number on the inside that I don't know what it means. Do you?"

"Probably. Tell me the number and I'll see." Serial numbers for service members were handed out somewhat sequentially, possibly offering a small piece of information.

Marybeth had jotted down the numbers before she left the house hoping he would ask.

"52-431-872"

"What!? Is this some sort of joke Marybeth, because if it is, it's not very funny."

Marybeth was stunned. She fumbled for words. "N-n-n-o-o-o-o, Dad. No. Why? What did I say? Oh my god, did I do something wrong?" She completely reverted to his little girl who was about to get into trouble for something.

There was silence on the other end of the phone. "I'm sorry, honey. Read the number again. I must have misheard you." His voice was eerily calm.

"52-431-872"

"And it's inside a helmet?"

"Yes, Dad. What does it mean?"

"It's my serial number and it means you've got my helmet from Vietnam."

They were both silent for an endless moment.

Marybeth looked at Josh, eyes wide with panic. He pulled the car over to the curb. To Josh, the disembodied voice on the phone was only a mumble but it sounded serious.

"Where did you get it?" Dad's voice was devoid of emotion and seemed to come from far away.

"At a yard sale yesterday. I'm sorry, Dad, I'm sorry. Are you okay?"

"I'm okay. I'm going to church now. And after that you are going to come over to my house with the stuff you have."

"Okay. Okay. Tell me what time to be there."

"11 o'clock."

"Okay. Dad, are you sure you're okay? And are you going to be okay till I get there? Maybe you should skip church and we can come right over?"

"We?" Sean immediately picked up on the plural pronoun.

"Yes, Josh is here. He got here yesterday."

"I'm okay and I will be okay. Church will help clear my head. Then we can talk. I expect it will be a long afternoon."

"Okay. We'll be there."

"Bye, honey."

"Bye, dad."

Marybeth sat in the car staring into nowhere holding her breath.

"MB! Are you okay? What the hell just happened?" Josh's voice was on the edge of panic.

"You're not going to believe this." She tried to catch a breath. "It's my dad's helmet."

They both sat silently, as if suspended in time and space, barely breathing, while their brains scrambled to add this information to the puzzle. Finally, Josh started up the car and pulled away from the curb.

"Where are we going?"

"To the diner. We need food."

"Is that your answer to everything?" she said, trying to add a little levity.

"Not the answer. But it's usually my first step." Seeing as Marybeth didn't have a better idea, she went along for the ride.

They rode in silence, got out of the car in silence and entered the diner in silence.

"Two?" the hostess asked.

Josh managed a nod and they were seated. They sat across the table staring at each other. Neither one knowing what to say next.

It was Marybeth who took the first deep breath. "Well, that went well, don't you think?"

They both let out a nervous laugh just as the waitress came over.

"Good morning. My name is Cindy and I'll be your waitress," she said looking down at her order pad. "Can I get you something to drink?"

"Coffee," they both said simultaneously.

"Got it." She handed them menus and went to retrieve the beverages that would sooth their nerves.

"What are we going to do?" asked Marybeth.

"Huh?" Josh said, looking over the menu.

"What do you mean, huh?" she said irritated again.

"I thought we were going to have breakfast and then go talk to your dad. Did I miss something?"

"I mean after that."

"After that depends on what your dad says." Josh replied, still not sure he was following the conversation.

Suddenly Marybeth's expression shifted as some new thought came into her mind. "Oh no!" she said.

"What now?"

"I totally forgot about the shop! Angie will be expecting me with a carload of goods at ten o'clock."

"So, just call her and tell her I'm in town and you're taking the day off?"

"She knows when I'm lying."

"You won't be lying."

"She'll know there's something else."

"Is she a mind reader?"

"No, she's a human lie detector."

"Just call her now and let her know." Josh encouraged. "It will be fine."

"Okay. But you'll see."

Marybeth dug the phone out of her purse and dialed Angie's home number. She put the phone on speaker.

"Hello, MB. What's up?" Angie answered the phone.

"Hi Angie. How's it going?"

"What's wrong?" Angie's antenna went up quick.

"Well, Josh came in a few days early and I was wondering if you can handle things at the shop today by yourself."

37

"Of course I can. What's wrong?"

"Nothing."

"Why is Josh here early?" she insisted.

"No reason." Marybeth tried to sound blasé.

"Okay, I'll go with that for now, but you better have the real story by tomorrow."

"Alright, Angie. I promise. Thanks a million."

Marybeth hung up the phone and turned to Josh. "I told you so."

Chapter 7

Sean's mind was racing. He was pacing the floor in his kitchen, waving his hands and talking to the air. "What the hell is going on? Is this some kind of joke? I'm sorry Bobby. I couldn't get to you. There was nothing I could do. I tried. Even after I left Vietnam, I tried. But the magic was gone. I'm sorry." Suddenly and without warning Sean found himself in one of those flashback moments that he hadn't had in years.

He was at the forward collection point. US troops were suffering high casualties and he had been sent forward to a place where bodies were brought in from the front lines. Here they would be "bagged and tagged" and transported to Danang by helicopter or truck, to the mortuary there, where he was usually stationed. Danang was relatively safe and he sometimes felt guilty for that. Now, here he was closer to the war and he was scared.

Choppers were landing at a steady pace, literally dumping bodies out and taking off again. He did his best to line them up and in some cases piece them together like macabre puzzles. Then he would start the paperwork with whatever identification he could find, usually dog tags. All the while hearing shells and gunfire not so far away. He was surprised that even here, under such conditions, he could still hear the words of the dead. He did his best to write them down, fearing he might not get another chance in Danang when he got back, if he got back. He was moving down the line of corpses, when a familiar face stared blankly up at him. It was Bobby, still wearing Sean's helmet.

"Oh, no. Not you too Bobby. Shit. That helmet didn't do you much good, did it?" he said aloud.

"Don't worry Sean, it worked just fine," he heard in his head. Just then, a shell hit the collection point. Then another. Sean was hit.

When he came out of it, he was on the floor in his kitchen, sweating and breathing hard. "Fuck!" he screamed, "Not again, please God, not again." He got his bearings, climbed up to a kitchen chair and sat at the table, trembling. "I'm sorry, Bobby. I'm sorry I didn't get a chance to get a message to your family like I did for other guys. I tried, really." He rested his head in his hands. "And where did Marybeth get my helmet. It must have gone with you to the states. Are you coming back to haunt me? I thought this nightmare was over."

He knew from past experience that the best thing to do now was to stay quiet until his nerves calmed down and do something normal. After a minute or so he shook it off as best he could and got up to make himself another pot of coffee. Church this morning was definitely out. He couldn't be around a lot of people. He paced the kitchen floor for a few more minutes. He couldn't get the memory out of his head. For the first time in more than 20 years, he wanted a drink.

Getting sober was the hardest thing he'd ever done. It was the combination of treatment and Alcoholics Anonymous, AA for short, that pulled him through some very grueling years. A lot of vets found themselves looking for help in the years after the war. The AA meetings were full of them. He had a sponsor, which is part of how the program works, but he hadn't talked to him in months, maybe even a year or more. He was counting on him being home when he picked up the phone. He dialed the number from memory.

"Hey, Adam. It's me Sean. I know it's been a while."

"Sure has, buddy. You okay? Because you don't sound it."

"I'm sober if that's what you mean, but I sure could use a little support if you've got the time. I got a real kick in the gut this morning."

"Sure thing. You want to talk on the phone or get together?"

"I probably should get out of the house. Can you meet me at the Donut Hole for coffee?"

"Be there in ten." Adam knew this was serious. Sean wasn't one to pull the alarm for nothing.

"Thanks, Adam."

"Don't mention it."

The Donut Hole was a local haunt used as a meeting place for all manner of social and community groups. On Mondays it was the after meeting for a nearby AA group. Tuesdays you could find the Book Nook book club there. The shop even had its own softball team. They, however, went to the local pub after the games. Today, Sunday, brought in the after-church crowd around ten or so, but now the place was quiet.

It had been a regular spot for Sean and Adam to meet in Sean's early days in recovery. It had that comfortably familiar feeling as Sean pulled into the parking lot. It helped to calm his nerves a little more.

He spotted Adam in a corner booth and slid in opposite him.

"What's up Sean? You look like hell."

"Yeah. Well, wait till you hear the story. My daughter called this morning..."

Adam waved a hand at him. "Wait. Wait. Why don't you start easy, by catching me up on what's been happening since we last talked?"

"Okay. Good idea." Sean took a deep breath. "Well, I'm still together with Sue. Still retired and loving it. My youngest, Regina, moved in with her boyfriend and has started doing stand-up comedy in Philly."

"Really?"

"Yeah. She's pretty good too, although she gets a lot of her material from her family." Sean shrugged his shoulders with a smile.

Adam chuckled. "I'll bet she does. I'm sure it helps you to keep it real."

"It sure does. I'll admit, laughing about things puts it in perspective. Humor therapy I call it."

"I can imagine that's true." Adam was nodding and smiling.

"Marybeth's shop is doing great. She loves it. And she's got herself a new guy, Josh, who lives in Connecticut."

"300 miles. Probably works really well for her."

"Yeah. I will say though, that she's softened a lot over the past year. We had a couple of good conversations last fall, let out some secrets I guess you could say, and things have been good."

Sean was feeling a sense of normal settling back over his world. "How are you doing? We should really get together with you and Bonnie soon. Are you going to the Jack-O-Lantern Festival?"

"We are. We're bringing the grandchildren."

"Oh, God. How old are they now?"

"Four and six. Hard to believe. They want to carve pumpkins for the festival. Bonnie told them they could draw the faces and she would do the cutting."

"Good plan. Well, maybe Sue and I can meet you there."

"Sounds good. So now tell me what's going on."

"Now that I'm a little calmer, I'm going to start at the beginning. In Vietnam."

"Holy shit, Sean. You're digging up the *old* bones. I've never heard you say more than three words about your time in the service."

"Yeah. And I would have been happy to continue with that tradition but someone else has other plans."

"I have to let you know that I was just young enough to miss all that. I never even had to register for the draft. Maybe I'm not the one you should be talking to."

"You're the best one. This isn't about the war. It's about sobriety."

"Sure. Okay. Tell me your story."

Sean went on to tell Adam about Bobby, the voices of the dead, and the festering guilt he had been harboring for all these years.

Adam sat quietly, listening and nodding his head. When Sean was finished Adam waited a moment and then, without batting an eye he said "So, aside from the unusual particulars of your story, what's got you so worked up."

43

"Marybeth called me this morning. She picked up a few army things at a yard sale and wants me to take a look at them. One of the items is my helmet."

"Are you sure?" Adam asked incredulously.

"Pretty sure, without actually looking at it."

"How is that possible?"

"I don't know, but it sent me into a flashback this morning like I haven't had in years."

"Ah. That's why you called."

"Yup."

"What are you afraid of?" It was a standard AA question when someone was having a hard time.

"Are you kidding? I have a list going. Like "Is Bobby coming back to haunt me? How did my daughter get my helmet? Are the flashbacks going to start up again?"

"So, what's the antidote to fear?" Again, it was a question right out of the recovery books.

"Faith." It was a standard answer.

"And what or who do you need to have faith in?"

"In myself for starters, I guess. Faith that I can handle this without drinking or going crazy."

"Good start." Adam gave him a nod. "What else do you need?"

"I need more information," Sean said thoughtfully.

"How are you going to get it?"

"I guess my daughter will supply some, but that brings up more fear. What if she thinks I'm crazy?"

"Sean, we all think you're crazy," Adam said with a smile.

"This is different. This is my daughter."

"This is not different. This is your ego telling you this is different. Your daughter loves you. No matter what."

Sean paused, thinking about these words. "Yeah, I know. But what if she thinks less of me somehow?"

"Sean?" Adam looked serious. "Have you ever told anyone this story before?"

"No."

"Ah, that explains a lot. Listen, trust me, you need to tell your daughter the whole story and you need to listen to what she has to say to you about this helmet thing. Everything else will work out."

"You sound so sure."

"Sean, you have to tell your story. Let the secrets out."

"You're right," Sean acquiesced. "We're only as sick as the secrets we keep." It was one of the many saying from AA. He took a deep breath for the first time since the phone call. "I just needed a little perspective and you're usually the guy that can give it to me."

"My pleasure. Are you feeling a little clearer?"

"Yeah. For the moment. But I reserve the right to call you again if I lose my focus."

"Not a problem. If nothing else, let's meet up on Saturday at the festival and you can catch me up."

They finalized plans and Sean headed home.

Chapter 8

Marybeth and Josh were back at the house. Breakfast had been a relatively quiet affair with both of them floating in and out of quiet reflection. Now they were comfortably seated in the living room, each with a computer on their lap. Josh always brought his laptop with him knowing that he would write for at least a few hours during his trip. At the moment, they were surfing the web, looking for information about the Vietnam War and the home-front.

"Let's see," Josh was thinking out loud. "We know his first name and we know when his last entry into his journal was, April 4, 1970. I would have to assume that was the day he died, or close seeing as his entries were fairly regular. I wonder what I can find with that."

"Lots of luck. I'll start at my favorite site, Wikipedia, and see what info might be useful."

They both tapped away at their keys, reading, then tapping some more.

"Oh my god," Josh exclaimed. "I found a list of Vietnam deaths in alphabetical order. I don't have a last name. I suppose the first name would be listed as Robert but that doesn't help." He continued to scroll. "I can't search by date but MB! It's seventy-one single-spaced pages! Soldiers must have been dying by the thousands."

Marybeth didn't look up from her screen. "According to Wikipedia," she said solemnly, "6,137 soldiers died in 1970. If I do the math," she tapped a few keys, "that's 515 each month assuming it's spread out evenly across the year." Tap, tap, tap. "That's 17 a day, every day, including the weekends."

They both looked at each other in shock. "My father told me his job was to process the dead."

"That's a lot of dead." Josh shook his head in amazement.

"Oh my God!" Marybeth's eyes got bigger as she kept reading. "Apparently, the progress of the war was measured in body counts. The highest day of losses for U S troops being January 31, 1968 with 246 dead." Marybeth felt a weight heavy on her chest. "Dad told me he had an odd habit of keeping count of the number of bodies he handled. I remember it was a high number, but I didn't really think about it at the time," she paused.

"Well, if he served with Robert, he might have been over there during that time."

"According to this other site, one of the major news networks started their program each night with the daily count of dead Americans. It is credited with fueling the already growing opposition movement."

"I can see that. With those numbers, I'd probably be out protesting too."

"When Dad got back, he got involved in the protests. That's where he met my mom." Marybeth physically shook off the alarming numbers. "Anyway, he married my mother in 1971. That means he finished up his tour in Vietnam in 1970. It looks like Robert and my dad were over there at the same time.

Do you think my dad knew him or maybe processed his body or something?"

"Could be," Josh nodded.

"Wow. This is all getting freakishly real. I wish I had waited to say anything until we looked into it more."

"My mother's cards said that it would be a time of healing life's wounds and resolving old issues. I have to believe this will all turn out the best for everyone."

"I sure hope you're right." Marybeth thought about her dad and glanced up at the clock. "It's a bit early but maybe we should head over to dad's and be there when he gets home from church?"

"Good idea." Josh took a deep breath. "Besides, I don't think I can do much more of this research right now."

"Yeah. Me either."

Marybeth and Josh pulled up just after 10:30. Marybeth was a wreck worrying about her dad. They were surprised to see Sean's car in the driveway. They expected he would still be at church. This just added to Marybeth's panic. She jumped out of the car and charged into the house.

"Dad? Dad? Where are you? Are you okay?"

"I'm in here," came a voice from the kitchen.

Marybeth raced around the corner. "Are you okay?"

Sean was sitting at the kitchen table drinking coffee. "Yes, honey. I'm fine, just a little off balance by your yard sale find, so stop panicking. When did you become such a Nervous Nellie?" He was doing his best to stay calm, for his own good as well as for Marybeth.

"Always. I've always been like this."

"Oh yeah. Now I remember."

"And I've been going crazy ever since we talked. What are you doing home? Did you miss church?"

"I decided to stay home this morning and steady myself for whatever drama you have cooked up," he said, trying to make light of the situation.

"I haven't cooked up anything. No drama. Really," she said hastily, knowing it was a lie.

"I'll be the judge of that," he kidded. "Now let me see what it is you've found."

"Well," she hesitated, "first maybe I should explain a few things."

"Not now, Marybeth, just let me see what you have."

He had that tone about him and Marybeth knew she was not going to get around it. She was worried that he might have some strange experience handling the helmet and had planned on telling him about the events of last year to give him a warning. But he could be very insistent so all she could do was hope for the best.

"Josh is bringing them in."

Josh came through the kitchen doorway carrying a canvas bag.

"Let me have it." Marybeth instructed him.

He hesitated. "Are you sure?" He knew this was not part of their carefully constructed plan to ensure Sean's safety.

"Yes, Dad has that 'Don't argue with me, little girl' tone."

"Okay," Josh said as he handed the bag over to her.

"Dad, I really wish you'd let me explain a few things first," she said, trying to slow down the whole process.

"Really, Marybeth, I'm fine."

She slowly took the helmet out of the bag and gingerly handed it to him.

As soon as the helmet hit his hands Sean heard Bobby in his head.

Hey Sean, it's me Bobby.

He jumped a bit causing him to juggle the helmet for a moment.

"Dad, are you okay?" Marybeth's panic was back on the rise.

"Be quiet please, Marybeth," he said sternly.

Hey Sean, you okay? he heard in his head.

Silently he replied, "Yes, Bobby. I'm fine. Just a little surprised. What's going on? Are you haunting me or something?"

Heck no, you knucklehead. I need your help. Fast.

"What could I possibly do for you? Deliver that last message to your wife? I have always felt really bad about that."

No. No. Nothing like that. I hope you haven't spent the last 40 years worrying about that?

"Well, actually, I have always felt really bad about it. Like I let you down when it really counted."

Aaawwwweee. Sean. For Pete's sake! I saw you get blown up! I know you didn't just walk away from me. How's that knee by the way?

"Great. Good as new. In fact, it is new, just last year."

Wow. They're doing amazing things now-a-days.

"Nonetheless, Bobby. I've always felt like I let you down. I wish I could have gotten a message to your wife. I suppose it's not too late."

Well, interesting you should say, Sean. See, I need your help. That's why I'm here.

"Anything, Bobby. If it's in my power to do, consider it done."

51

It's my son, James. He just retired from the army. He did two tours in Iraq and one in Afghanistan. He's messed up, Sean. He's thinking about blowin' his brains out.

"Shit, Bobby! Shit. Where is he?"

Well, that's the thing. I don't know. I only know he's in trouble. You gotta help him, Sean. You gotta do this for me.

"Sure, Bobby. Sure, but..."

I gotta go now.

"Wait. Wait." Sean was calling out loud.

"Wait what? Wait who?" Marybeth asked nervously.

Sean looked up to see Marybeth and Josh staring at him. He shook his head as if to clear out cobwebs.

"Shit," he said, looking at them both. "I need a cup of coffee." He started to get up.

"I'll get it." Marybeth jumped up, grabbed his mug and headed to the counter. "I need one too. How 'bout you, Josh?"

"None for me, thanks."

With her back to them she continued. "We are worried sick about you, Dad."

"Well, put your mind at ease. I'm really okay."

"Really? Then suppose you tell me what just happened." She turned and handed him his coffee.

"It's complicated. I have my own story to tell, but first you have a story for me. You can start by telling me where you got this helmet."

"Okay, but I have to tell you a different story first." She sat back down, then looked at Josh for support. He gave her a smile and a nod of encouragement.

Sean noticed the nod. "I was right. It's going to be a long afternoon," Sean said as he settled back into his chair.

Marybeth took a long deep breath and then began the story of the unusual yard sale last year that appeared to be hosted by a ghost. She told him about the visions and strange items she had acquired. She thought she was done with all that craziness and was putting it all behind her when the sign appeared again yesterday. When she got there, the old woman was nowhere to be found. Standing on the porch was a mysterious army man who pleaded with her to help him.

"He wanted me to get the helmet to "him" and that I would know what to do." She paused, then, hearing nothing but silence, she immediately jumped back in. "You don't think I'm crazy, do you?"

Sean smiled, realizing that his own fear just an hour ago had been the opposite, that she would think him crazy.

"No, honey. I don't think you're crazy at all."

"Why don't you think I'm crazy? Because I think I'm crazy."

"Let's just say, if you're crazy so am I. And I'm reasonably sure I'm not."

She studied him for a moment. "I had no idea at the time who 'him' was but I'm starting to think it's you."

"Yes," he paused, "It's me." He knew that he would have to tell his own story soon enough.

"Oh no! What is happening? My head is spinning from all this and I'm worried sick about you on top of it all. Are you okay? What happened when you touched the helmet?"

"Well, like you, in order to tell you that story, I have to tell you a different story first."

Sean took a long drink of his coffee. Marybeth and Josh sat quietly and waited for Sean to say what he needed to say.

"When I was in Nam, I was stationed at the Danang Mortuary, processing the remains of soldiers killed in action. When I was there, something strange happened to me. I suddenly had, or was granted, or developed, or something, an ability to talk to the dead." He paused here to gauge the audience. He noticed a raised eyebrow from Marybeth, but after seeing no particular distress at this announcement, he went on.

"As I was doing the paperwork for individuals, I would ask them if there were any last words they wanted me to convey to their families. Often, I would hear the soldier in my head telling me some message. Anyway, one day Bobby comes into camp with his unit to restock supplies. He sat down with me at lunch and we struck up a conversation. He told me that he could tell if someone was dead in the field by a vapor that he could see hovering over their body. He thought maybe it was their soul or something. He never told anyone about it. He saw me out in the compound that day processing bodies and he could see the vapors floating up to heaven when I was done with them. He asked me about it. I told him about hearing people's last messages to family. Then the sergeant came through dining hall and sent us back to work. It wasn't much of a conversation, really, but it had a big effect on me. For the first time, I felt like I wasn't crazy. I think it meant a lot to him too."

"It did, Dad. He said you eased his burden that day and that he never got to thank you for it."

"Well, he eased mine a lot, too. Anyway, the following morning I saw him loading up his truck and getting ready to pull out. Things had changed overnight, and their three-day respite was cut off. They were heading back out immediately. His truck was pulling out of the yard when he realized he had left his helmet at the dining hall. He started panicking about not having time to go back and get it, so I gave him mine, thinking I didn't really need it in Danang which was fairly secure. He said thanks and told me to use his until he got back." Sean stopped for a moment, lost in thought.

"That's how he got your helmet." Marybeth commented.

"Yes," he said, coming out of his reflections. "The fighting got worse over the next two days and bodies were getting backed up at the forward collection point, so they sent me out to help. I had already seen a lot of horror from the safety of the mortuary, but it wasn't anything compared to what I saw at the collection point. When I got there, the place was in chaos. Choppers landing everywhere unloading both wounded and dead soldiers or what was left of them. Supplies were low, people were scrambling everywhere. I didn't know what to do so I just jumped in, helping the living and processing the dead, writing notes on blank paper that would eventually become a letter to the family about where and how they died. I'd been working steady for seven hours and still the bodies kept coming. Some had missing limbs, some were in pieces.

I was working my way down a line of corpses when I came across Bobby's body. He had a hole in his chest the size of my fist. He was still wearing my helmet. Before I could start my note, the station came under attack with artillery. One went off just to the left of me and threw me into the air. I landed hard on the ground with shrapnel all over my left side. Laying there, I realized I had become one of the wounded and wondered if I would become one of the dead. Everyone who was able helped load wounded and dead back onto choppers and sent them directly to Danang. I flew back with eight bodies and two other wounded soldiers." Sean took a deep breath and shook his head as if trying to erase some mental picture.

"Turned out I wasn't as bad as I looked but I still needed knee surgery right away. My initial tour had been over for two months already so they sent me stateside where they did the surgery, then gave me a purple heart and discharge papers. I never got a chance to hear what Bobby had to say. No message for his wife and son. I've felt bad about that for all these years."

Sean paused for a moment to catch his breath and shake off the memories.

"Wow, Sean." Josh's voice was low. "I don't even know what to say to that."

"There isn't much to say. It was what it was." There was another long pause.

Then Marybeth jumped in. "'*Was* being the operative word here. It's over, Dad. In the past."

"Yes, until now," replied Sean.

"What do you mean?" Marybeth asked with concern.

"Well, I just had a conversation with Bobby when I picked up the helmet."

Another moment of silence settled over the room.

"What did he say?" Josh asked.

"He said his son is in trouble and that I have to stop him from killing himself."

"Oh, no. Would that be James?" asked Marybeth.

Sean looked at her with raised eyebrow.

"We read the letters hoping to find out some information," she offered apologetically, "and the baby was in my vision."

"Was there anything else in the letters?" Sean asked hopefully.

"No, just forty-year-old love letters basically," supplied Josh. "Did Bobby tell you where to find this boy."

"Not boy, Josh. James is forty and just retired from the army. He saw combat in both Iraq and Afghanistan."

"Shit!" said Josh as he let out a breath.

"Yeah. That's what I said," added Sean.

"Well, where is he? Let's go get him." Marybeth was ready to go.

"Bobby didn't know where he was."

"How could he not know!? He's dead! Don't dead people know those kinds of things?" Marybeth demanded.

"All I can say," Sean said calmly, "is apparently not. Bobby was gone before I could ask him anything else."

Everyone sat there quietly for a moment, considering all the information that had just been presented.

"What do we do now?" asked Marybeth.

"I suggest we get something to eat." It was Josh, of course, ever the pragmatist.

"Really, Josh? Is that the best you can come up with?" Marybeth complained.

"Josh is right," her dad agreed.

"Really?" Marybeth feigned betrayal.

"It's nearly two o'clock Marybeth and, I don't know about you, but I haven't eaten since nine. My brain needs food to think best. We need to get up, walk around, get out of the house and step away from all this for the moment." Sean's authoritative tone gently took over the situation and plans were made to go get lunch.

Chapter 9

They decided on pizza. It seemed easy and fast. They took separate cars. Sean insisted that he needed a little quiet time to let things settle. Marybeth and Josh were already seated and reviewing the menu when he arrived.

"I suggest that we talk about other things besides the weekend's events. That way we can get a little distance from things," he said as he joined them.

"Okay," agreed Marybeth. "First topic of discussion, then, is what do you want on your pizza?"

"Everything and anything, so you two decide."

"Mushrooms, sausage, pepperoni and extra cheese," announced Josh.

"And broccoli," added Marybeth.

Josh and Sean both looked at her as if she were an alien.

"It must include something green," she defended her position.

"How about green peppers," Josh offered as an alternative.

"Okay."

Josh headed up to the counter to place the order.

"I know you don't want to talk about things, but I just need to check in with you to make sure you're okay, you know, mentally or emotionally or whatever." Marybeth felt awkward around the subject of her father's mental health.

"Yes, honey. Thanks for asking and I'm fine, really. I called a friend of mine this morning and talked a few things out."

"One of the AVs?" she asked referring to the nickname he had given his Army Vet group.

"No. My AA sponsor, if you must know, Miss Nosy Rosy," he teased.

"Oh, no, Dad. Not that?"

"No, not really. He's just a really good reality check for me and he was very helpful this morning. Stop worrying. I have my own support system in place."

Just then Josh returned to the table with an order number and some drinks.

"Alright, what did I miss?"

"Dad was just telling me about his band of merry men, the AVs."

"What's that?"

"It's a name I gave my new group of old friends from the VA, Army Vets, AVs."

"It sounds very official."

"Not really, but we are starting to organize a few events and presentations, unofficially, to raise awareness of Veterans' issues. So, next weekend we are setting up a small table outside the grocery store to reach out to vets and their families who might not ever go to the VA. The truth is, going to the VA center can be a trigger for vets."

"Really?" Josh was surprised. "How's that? That's where they have to go for help, isn't it?"

"Yes. It doesn't seem like it would make sense, does it? But seeing a bunch of men and women in uniform and hearing all the military jargon can send some people into anxiety attacks or flashbacks."

"Wow, that's got to make it hard for people to get the help that they need?" Josh was still trying to figure this out.

"Yes, it does. So, we are hoping that by being visible, in civilian clothes, offering unofficial assistance, we can spare someone years of distress trying to do it on their own."

"Dad, are you sure that's the best idea considering recent events?" Marybeth chimed in.

"Getting back in touch with these guys has been nothing but great for me and I expect it to continue that way, so stop worrying about me. Honestly Marybeth, how many times do I have to say that?" Sean looked at Marybeth sternly. The question was starting to irritate him.

"Okay. Okay. I get it," she conceded. Just then, the pizza arrived and they all dug in, hungrier than they thought.

Sean changed the subject. "So, you two are coming up on one year. How's the long-distance thing going?

"Really, Dad?" Marybeth was defensive. "How do you even remember that? Are you charting our relationship on the kitchen calendar?"

Sean held up his hands. "Take it easy, Marybeth. You guys got together at the Jack-O-Lantern Festival and here it is, coming around again. I'm not crossing boundaries here. Just noticing."

"Oh, right."

Josh jumped in. "Yes, Sean, it is one year and thank you for remembering." He took Marybeth's hand and smiled at her. "We haven't really talked about it much. However, we do have plans to celebrate at the Crabby Apple."

"How appropriate," Dad ribbed.

"And pumpkin carving, if you must know," Marybeth added sourly. "Now can we talk about something else? Are you contributing a pumpkin or two this year for the new World Record?"

The Jack-o-Lantern Festival had become known for breaking the Guinness World Book of Records for the most lighted jack-o-lanterns in one spot at one time.

"Of course. Sue and I will be doing our part again this year. We're upping our contribution from two to three. And you?"

"We'll be happy to get two out this year without any blood loss." Josh joked. "Besides, I have some deadlines for my book that will take up any spare time."

"Oh, yeah. What's happening with that?"

Josh had just finished a manuscript for a youth novel about growing up different. It came out of his own experience as a kid who was often looked at as a freak or strange by his classmates. It was a hard story to write but the finished product showed sincerity and understanding. The publisher loved it.

"Wow. That's quite an accomplishment. Congratulations." Sean was impressed.

"Thanks."

They continued to exchange pleasantries, happy to have a break from the morning's drama. They all knew it would come around again soon enough. Before they knew it, the pizza was gone and there was a lull in the conversation as the busboy came by to retrieve the empty pan.

"So, what's our next move with all this?" Marybeth started off.

"Well, first of all it's not "our" move. It's "my" move. This is my problem now," Sean corrected her.

"Oh no you don't," Marybeth shot back quickly. "My yard sale, my task."

"Hardly. You have passed the baton, so to speak, and now it's mine."

Josh butted in, "Really? Guys... Hold up!"

They both looked at him in surprise.

He continued, "Look, there is plenty to do if we are going to find this man quickly. So, let's try to define what needs to be done and who is best to do it. We can all help."

They looked at Josh, then at each other. "Alright," they both agreed.

Josh took over from here. "We need to find this man's son, James. What was Bobby's last name?"

Sean hesitated, "I've been wracking my brains all morning and it's right on the tip of my tongue. McIntyre, McCarthy, McGinnis. I just can't remember."

"Great!" Marybeth said, frustrated already.

"Look, I'm doing the best I can. Can you offer any other information?" he asked defensively.

"No."

"Then help work on the solution, please."

"So, what do we know?" asked Josh.

"We know that you swapped helmets forty years ago, half way around the world, with a guy you hardly knew," supplied Marybeth.

"Thanks for that," Sean replied.

"Wait," Josh jumped in. "If he had your helmet, do you still have his?"

"I don't know. Why?"

"Well, if his helmet had your serial number in it, will yours have his number?"

"Wow. Good thinking. I honestly don't know if I still have it. I have an old footlocker stuffed with whatever I have from back then."

"Where is it?" Marybeth asked with renewed optimism.

"It's at the house."

"Let's go," Marybeth said as she started to get up.

"Hold your horses, there, little girl," Sean stopped her. "I might have to take this thing a little slower than you would like. I'm not sure I have it in me today to open that thing up."

"Okay," Marybeth resumed her seat, remembering her dad's PTSD. "What do you propose? Josh and I could have a look?"

"No. I just need some time to get ready for all this. I think I'd like to have one of the AV guys with me when I open it up. Let me call someone and see if they can come over tomorrow."

Marybeth started to protest but caught herself. "Okay. Is there anything we can do to be helpful?"

"Well, let's start looking at what else we know and what we can find out. Just having a serial number might not get us anywhere either. It's not like I can just call up the Army and ask for information about an old serial number," Sean pointed out.

"Great." Marybeth slumped back in the booth. "So, what else do we know?"

Sean got solemn, "We know the date that he died. April 5th, 1970."

"I found that website with the names from the war in alphabetical order. I can continue to look for something in chronological order," Josh said. "Then search for anyone named Robert or Bobby."

Marybeth thought for a moment. "I can try to track down Becky and James by doing some research on what happens to military families when their soldier dies? Do they get to stay on post? Do they have to move? What about benefits for the surviving children?" She looked at her dad for any information.

"I have no idea about that stuff," he said, shrugging his shoulders. "Did you get anything at all from the letters, now that we have some idea what we're looking for?"

Marybeth shook her head. "Not that I can think of, but it would be worth reading them again along with the journal to see if there are any identifiers about where they lived before the army or where their families might have been."

"Great. Why don't you two chip away at that stuff. I'll call my VA buddies and see if they have any other ideas or want to help, which I'm sure they will. How about if we touch base tomorrow at noon to see where we are with things?"

"Okay," Marybeth agreed. "I won't ask you if you're going to be okay, but are you?"

Sean got up to leave. "Yes. See you tomorrow sometime." He leaned over and kissed her on the forehead. "Call me if you find out anything important."

"See ya, Sean." Josh shook his hand as he left.

Marybeth looked at Josh. "Suddenly, I'm exhausted."

"Yeah, me too. Let's go home."

Chapter 10

It was late afternoon when Sean got back to his house. Long shadows of the setting sun stretched across his kitchen, reminding him of the explosion forty years ago. These were the kinds of everyday things that coaxed memories back into consciousness. He had been exhausted that afternoon back in Nam, just as he was at this moment. Maybe if he hadn't been so tired that day, he could have reacted faster, ran for cover, helped Bobby to say good bye. How many times had he played it over in his head, different ways, different decisions, imagining that he could have caused a different outcome? Even while he was rehashing the events, he realized he was tired of doing it, tired of imagining how his life would have been different if only. . .

The helmet was still sitting on the table. He stood staring at it, frozen, numb, recalling the words Bobby had spoken just this morning. "I hope you haven't spent the last forty years worrying about that?" Truth was, he had. But now he was wondering himself why he had chosen to focus on that one missed conversation for so many years. In the scheme of things, it was not the worst thing he'd seen in Nam, not by a long shot. We are only as sick as the secrets we keep. Maybe that's what this is about. This whole piece of his service, the voices, the conversation with Bobby at lunch that day, the vapors Bobby saw. Had it all been a dirty little secret that had kept him sick? He'd never told anyone. But why? Now that it had been said out loud today, it didn't seem like much at all, and certainly not in light of Marybeth's story.

Just then, there was a knock at the door and Marybeth let herself in. "Hey," she said on her way into the kitchen. "Just remembered that we left the helmet and letters," she gestured to the table. Hanging on the back of one of the kitchen chairs was the tote bag with the letters and journal bundled together with the twine. She noticed the vacant look on Sean's face. "If you're not okay, will you promise to call me?" she asked.

"If I'm not okay, I promise to call *someone.* It might not be you."

"I can live with that. Would you like me to leave the helmet or take it with me?" she asked.

"Leave it, if it's all the same to you."

"Fine. I'll take these, though." She reached out and grabbed the tote bag. "Call me tomorrow," she called over her shoulder as he headed out the door.

The interruption was enough to break Sean out of his reflections. "What now?" he thought. He sat at the table, turning the helmet over in his hands. He had been hesitant to pick it up at first, fearing Bobby would jump back into his head or maybe *hoping* that he would. He wasn't sure which. When he did pick it up, he found himself alone with his thoughts. Generally not much of a talker, he hesitated to call anyone, but recovery is about sharing the burden and getting some perspective. He picked up the phone.

"Hey, Ray," he said into the phone. "I've got a little bit of something going on and I'm wondering if you have some time to talk it out with me?"

"Sure. Of course. It sounds serious."

"Yeah," was all Sean could muster.

"On the phone or over coffee?"

"Over coffee if you can. My place?"

"Sure. I'll be there in 30 minutes."

"Thanks Ray."

Ray was one of his oldest friends. They met on the way to basic training and were in the same unit for a short time until Ray was assigned to civil engineers and Sean to medical. But they had gotten close quickly and stayed in touch during the war as best they could. Afterward, there had been so much chaos and upheaval at home that they lost contact for a while, then met back up at VVAW, Vietnam Vets Against the War. It was a grass roots movement that developed back in the 70's to assist vets with all kinds of things. Again, they stayed in touch for a time, but then life got busy. When Sean had gone back to the VA hospital last year for counseling, he ran into Ray again. They immediately reconnected and started getting together for coffee. At first, they chatted about life and events of the intervening years. After a few weeks they cautiously allowed the conversation to gravitate to the war. It seemed that forty years was just about the right amount of time to start talking about what had happened to them over there. They shared bits and pieces, meeting at the VA coffee shop regularly. Over time they bumped into a few other guys that they knew from the war, or from the VVAW. Now numbering six, they became a little band of brothers in a way, cautiously talking about things that no one ever talked about. Sean was glad Ray could come over. In Sean's mind, Ray seemed the most likely to understand the stories Sean had to tell.

After putting on a pot of coffee, he moved the helmet to the coffee table and headed to the attic. The access was one of those pull-down-from-the-ceiling staircases in the second-floor hallway. He hadn't been up there in years and his recollection of it being organized proved to be a slight exaggeration. The trunk was over in the corner, near boxes of old tax records. He'd moved it around a bit over the years, but he hadn't opened it since before he got married. He really couldn't remember what was in there anymore, besides demons and ghosts.

He spent a few minutes clearing a path from the footlocker to the drop-down stairs and then carefully dragged it down to the living room. He was brushing the dust off when the doorbell rang.

It was Ray, standing on the stoop wearing his usual cowboy hat, jeans and boots. Ray liked the western cowboy look despite their northern location and Sean had to admit that he wore it well. Ray put his hat and keys down on the table by the door as he came in. "What's going on, Sean?"

"Hey, Ray, thanks for coming over."

"No problem, man. You sounded intense."

"You don't know the half of it."

Ray's eyebrows raised as he noticed the footlocker. "Well, buddy, is that the half I don't know?"

"It is and it isn't. Let's just say that I have some stuff I need to do, I need to do it now and I'd rather not do it alone."

"Alright then, soldier. Tell me what you need."

"I have coffee on. This could take a while."

Sean and Ray headed for the kitchen where they sat for a while as Sean began to tell the old story of Bobby and the vapors, the voices and the helmet. He told him about the guilt for not giving Bobby his chance at last words. The whole time, Ray sat quiet and let Sean have his say. When he was finished, Sean looked at Ray for some comment.

"Well, that's quite a story. I got two things for you. One, is that you and Bobby are not the only ones that had strange things happen to you over there. I remember one time in particular, we were out on patrol and a buddy was about twenty feet ahead of me on this trail. Suddenly, he turned to me with an "oh, shit" look on his face and I heard him plain as day in my head scream "RRRuuuuuunnnnn!" Now, mind you, I didn't *see* him say it. I just heard it in my head and I took him at his word. I took off the way I'd come just as the booby trap exploded. After that I always seemed to know when something was going to go wrong and avoided it, like hitting the ground just before the gunfire started, or changing direction for no reason only to find a booby trap in the path. I wasn't just being careful. I knew. I always thought it was that soldier looking out for me." Ray paused here waiting for some comment back.

"What's the second thing?" Sean asked.

"What second thing?" Ray looked confused.

"You said there were two things. What's the second thing?"

"Aaahhh," Ray shrugged. "I don't remember. This is the important one."

The both laughed. "It'll come to me later, I'm sure," Ray added, then, "So that's the old story. What's the new story? What's with the footlocker and the helmet?"

Sean took a deep breath. "It gets weirder from here."

"Hard to believe, but go on."

Sean took a deep breath. "My daughter called me this morning. She picked up a couple of military items at a yard sale and wanted to know if I could give her any information about them." Sean paused again.

71

"And?" Ray prompted.

"That helmet in there is one of them." They looked through the kitchen doorway into the living room where they could see the helmet, balanced upside down on the coffee table.

"Looks like Nam era from here," Ray said.

"It is. It's mine. It's the one I gave to Bobby."

"Okay, you're right. It is getting weirder."

"There's more."

"Shit. I need another cup of coffee for this." Ray got up and helped himself. "I don't suppose you got any whiskey?" he kidded, knowing that neither one of them drank anymore. He sat back down at the table. "Okay. Shoot."

"When I picked up the helmet, I heard Bobby's voice in my head, just like I did back then."

Ray took a deep breath. "What'd he say?"

"Among other things, he told me his son was in trouble and that I had to save him. His son just retired from the army after three combat tours and he's thinking about killing himself."

"Shit. Where is he?"

"Bobby didn't know."

"What do you mean he didn't know. He's dead. Don't dead people know things?"

Sean tried not to laugh as he heard Marybeth's words come at him again.

"Look, all I can say is he didn't. So, we have to find him."

"Okay. What's his name?"

"James."

"James what?"

"I don't know."

"Really?"

"Really."

"Shit."

"Yeah," Sean agreed. "So, the kids had an idea."

"Kids?" Ray interrupted.

"My daughter Marybeth and her boyfriend, Josh. Not really kids, I guess, but anyway...they thought that maybe I have Bobby's helmet in my old army stuff and if I do, maybe it has his serial number on it."

"And you didn't want to open it up by yourself." Ray stated it as a fact.

"Yeah."

"Are you ready to do it?"

"Not really, but I feel that time is not on our side."

"Probably not," Ray agreed. "You say when."

"Now," Sean said with a nod of his head.

Chapter 11

Marybeth and Josh were once again sitting in the living room researching the soldier and his family. Both were deep in thought. There was a comfortable silence between them that they had developed over the past year. Often Josh had to do a little work during their time together. Marybeth had learned that if Josh was writing, she needed to leave him alone and not interrupt him with every thought that entered her busy brain. It was difficult at first. In the past, silence usually meant an unresolved argument that would drag on for hours or days. She had gotten more comfortable with it as time went on. Today, they were both quietly engrossed in their tasks. While Josh was online reading about the war, Marybeth was rereading the letters Becky wrote to Bobby that she had retrieved from Dad's.

Josh found dozens of sites supporting veterans in a variety of ways; college funds, scholarships, advocacy, health care and so on. They all seemed to be focused on vets from the most recent conflicts in the middle east. Not much about supporting Vietnam veterans. There were a lot of sites about the war itself though.

"Oh my God, MB. Listen to this. 2.7 million Americans served in Vietnam from 1961 to 1973. One out of every 10 was a casualty. 58,148 were killed and 304,000 wounded, 75,000 severely disabled."

"Wow. My dad was one of the wounded."

"It says here on this site that, at the height of the war, 1968, 17,000 Americans died."

"What?" Marybeth tapped out the numbers on her computer. "If they were spread evenly over the entire year, that's 46 soldiers every day. That's crazy. I can almost see how my dad got fixated on the numbers. They're staggering."

"Yeah. I know almost nothing about the war. The site says the years of US troops on the ground were 1961 to 1973. That means I was eight when it was over."

"And I was three."

Josh's focus went back into the computer. Reading about it was almost spellbinding, like he was learning secrets about his own life. Clicking through to new links, he was shocked to read about marches on the capital. He knew there had been social unrest, sure, but he had no idea the scale. Hundreds of thousands of people protested the Vietnam War in cities all over the world. One of the largest was on October 21, 1967, when more than 100,000 protesters gathered at the Lincoln Memorial in Washington, DC. There were plenty of pro war demonstrations as well. Conservative America supported the administration's agenda to stop the spread of Communism.

He considered the current conflict in Iraq and Afghanistan. Although he didn't necessarily agree with it, he also never thought about standing up in opposition, certainly not marching on Washington, D.C. In fact, he hadn't heard of anyone else marching on Washington either. Was he really that self-centered or that disinterested? Was there an entire generation, maybe two, of apathy? These people in the 60s were taking over college campuses, demanding peace and riding buses against racism. That's passion! Where has all that gone? Thousands of people were recently slaughtered in the streets in Africa and it barely made the news. He felt a loss somewhere in the center of his being, a loss of his humanity maybe, disappointed in himself that he wasn't more aware and more vocal about the issues of his own time.

Meanwhile, Marybeth sat quietly reading through the letters, love letters really, from Becky to Bobby. She became more and more amazed at the depth of Becky's love. Marybeth realized that she had never felt that kind of love, not even early in her marriage, not even on her wedding day. She wondered if she was capable of it. Her marriage had wounded her so severely, she doubted that she had the capacity to love anyone again, at least not with such abandon as Becky. Trying to understand it, she reasoned that Becky and Bobby were so young, not much more than 18, that the ideal, hormone-fueled fantasy was in full bloom. But Becky's letters were more than that. It was as if Becky had accepted a piece of Bobby's soul to nurture and protect. How did she do it? Marybeth thought about her relationship with Josh. It was good, no doubt about it. It worked for them but sometimes she felt like she continued to stand just far enough off to walk away if needed. She danced around the edges and for now, Josh was okay with that. But she was sure he wanted more. In fact, he gave more than he got, even though he had a wound of his own to heal. Are some people just incapable of the depth of love that Becky had? Was she one of them?

"Hey," Josh called, startling Marybeth out of her contemplation, "there's a site for the Vietnam Veterans Against the War established in 1967. They were really active in the antiwar movement. That's pretty bold."

"That's them. The group my dad was with," she said, grateful to be pulled out of her reflections. "He said it was a crazy time. He told me about it last year. I think the protest at Arlington Cemetery, where he met my mom, might have been organized by them." She looked down at the letters. "Becky seemed to struggle between wanting to protest the war but wanting to be loyal to her husband who was tasked with fighting it. It felt like a contradiction to her. She said there were a fair amount of protests outside the base she was staying on, Fort Devens, somewhere in Massachusetts."

"Let me google it. Yeah, I've got it. Right here. It's about an hour and a half from my place in Connecticut. Established 1917...WWI and WWII...blah, blah, blah," he read aloud. "Says it was the deployment point for several brigades during the Vietnam War." He was gaining a little excitement thinking it could be the key, then sighed. "It says it's no longer open, closed in 1995. At least it verifies Becky's letters. Seems there were lots of protests outside the main gate."

"She says her family lives about two hours from her. How far is that?"

"Oh, hell. That would cover a lot of ground. My place is probably an hour and a half from there. So, you're talking about New Hampshire, Vermont, Massachusetts, Connecticut, Rhode Island and possibly New York and Maine."

"Seriously?" Marybeth asked in disbelief. She shook her head. "It doesn't seem like we're getting anywhere, does it?"

"Not yet maybe, but there's still lots of things to look for. Maybe there's some other clue. Keep reading."

They both returned to their tasks. Then, a moment later Josh leaned forward towards his computer. "Hey, I just hit pay dirt!

A site that lists deceased by date. It actually has photo images of the wall. This is great! What did your dad say the date was?"

"April 5th, 1970."

"Okay, here we go. Robert, Robert, Robert," he was saying aloud as he traced his finger down the page. "Oh my god. Here it is. Robert McMillan. That's got to be it. Died 4/5/1970."

They both looked at each other, somewhat shocked with their sleuthing success. Then there was silence as they tried to figure out what that meant.

"Great, but right now it just seems like more old information. It's not like we can call up the VA and ask about him." Marybeth cast the shroud of reality over their success.

"Right," Josh agreed.

"Try searching for Rebecca McMillan or his son, James McMillan."

"I'll put it in, but I'll probably get a thousand hits. And we don't even know if that's still their name. If Becky remarried and the new husband adopted him, it just got more complicated."

"In the vision I had, Bobby was pleading with Becky to find a good father for James, if he didn't come home." Marybeth's heart broke as she recalled the scene.

They continued their searches for another few minutes without success. Marybeth yawned and looked up at Josh who looked as tired as she felt. "Maybe we need to sleep on this and come at it fresh in the morning."

"Yeah, I'm good for calling it a day," Josh agreed. "We can call your dad in the morning and let him know we have a last name."

Chapter 12

Sean opened the foot locker to find two years of his life - horrific, fantastic, bizarre years - neatly packed away. They sat together on the couch unpacking the contents and spreading things across the coffee table and floor. Things were in neat piles, uniforms folded, paperwork in manila envelopes, letters tied up with string. He figured his mother must have packed it up when he was in rehab. There was no way Sean was this orderly. There was a small box filled with his ribbons and the brass insignia from his dress uniform. It was minus the Purple Heart. He had thrown that in the Potomac River during a protest in the 70's. He regretted it now but what's done is done. He knew he could replace it if he wanted to but it wouldn't be the same.

"Sometimes it's hard to believe, Ray, that we were really over there."

"I know what you mean. We were babies really, not even men yet. Drafted out of your poor mamma's arms."

"Yeah. I remember getting my orders to report for a physical a week after I registered. They didn't waste any time."

"In 1968 they were losing soldiers faster than they could sign them up." Ray was staring off in thought. "We're both lucky to have come back at all." He turned to Sean. "I don't know about you, but I didn't know what the fuck I was doing most of the time. I was just trying to stay alive."

"Yeah. I had it better than most, being in Danang, but still it seems unreal. Most days I felt like I was watching myself go through the motions." Sean moved a stack of tee shirts to reveal a helmet, nestled into the clothing below.

"Well, I'll be damned," Ray said when he spotted it.

Sean looked at Ray, then slowly removed the helmet from it's resting place. He sat quietly, turning the helmet over in his hands. He'd been wearing it when the bomb hit. Now, he ran his fingers over the dents in it from the explosion. It certainly had saved his life. Too bad his helmet hadn't saved Bobby's. He felt sick in his gut.

Ray broke the silence. "Well, it doesn't look like there's anything too scary in here to me. What do you think?"

"I think it's not what you can see that's scary. I think that war fucked me up for years," he said with bitter anger in his voice. "It changed everything. Changed the way I look at the world,"

"Everything that happens to us changes things, buddy. The war, marriage, divorce, addiction, recovery. Old age," he added with a bittersweet grin and a shrug of his shoulders. "I don't look at the world the same way I did ten years ago and that isn't because of the war."

"It was such an unbelievable fall from innocence for me. One minute I'm going to the prom, next minute I'm putting together horrible human jigsaw puzzles. Day in and day out. And they just kept coming. I was never done. I kept waiting for it to be done." Tears welled up in his eyes as he rolled the helmet over and over.

"War has never really been done," Ray pondered. "We just go from one to the next. Vietnam, Panama, Grenada, Kuwait, Iraq, Afghanistan and now looks like back to Korea again if this nut-job dictator over there doesn't accidentally get killed." Sean looked at Ray. He understood the reference. They both knew the US government was not beyond making accidents happen.

"You're right. Some days it just sneaks up on me. When I think about it too long, the guilt of coming home creates a physical pain in my chest, even now."

"A person can't ever know why things worked out the way they did over there. Maybe some of those guys wouldn't have been able to handle the stuff we came back to over here."

"That's true. It was no picnic. Sometimes I think that it was even worse than the war. At least over there, feeling like shit made sense. But here..." Sean let his thoughts trail off.

"Sometimes I wonder about the guys coming home now to a hero's welcome. I can get myself all worked up about the injustice of it all but sometimes I think maybe we had it easier."

"How can you possibly think that."

"These guys get a hero's welcome, come home with their units to lots of fanfare. Hell, dignitaries meet them coming off the planes. But, you know, being a hero is harder to live up to. We came home alone. We came home the bad guys, the villains. We wandered off back onto whatever life we left behind and did our best to lay low. At least that's what I did. We had to work our way back up to being respectable. But these guys today, they have a pedestal to maintain. The bar is really freakin' high. I'm guessing it's even harder for them to ask for help or show how messed up they are for fear of losing that glory. It can't be easy, Sean."

"I hadn't thought of it that way. There's probably some truth to that. Which brings us back around to the point of all this." He looked back down at the helmet. "I don't remember having this at the hospital, so it must have gone straight to my parents' house with my other personal items when I got med-evac'd out. That whole thing was a blur, even back then. So now, forty years later, I can hardly remember anything."

"We have to find Bobby's son. Now. So, we're going to have to shake some of that stuff loose from your brain if we're going to find him," Ray said, bringing the purpose of the task into full focus. "So, tell me what you do remember."

"Honestly, Ray. We didn't really talk that much. Just about the visions really. He told me how scared he was to be up in the fighting. He'd written a couple of letters home but didn't say anything about the war itself because he didn't want to upset his wife. Said she had enough to do with their son all by herself."

"Okay, so, she had no family?"

"None nearby I guess."

"Come on, man. Think. Anything else."

"Honestly, I don't think so. Maybe we should think of a different plan."

"Like what. All we got is a damn serial number!" Ray was clearly getting frustrated.

"Not *all* we have. We have Bobby's serial number. What can that get us?"

"Well, unless you have access to the military computers, it gets us nothing."

"Hey!" Sean shouted as an idea came into his head. "Doesn't Sammy go out with someone who works at the VA?"

"Yes," Ray nodded, "Yes, he does." He was wondering where this was going?

"Then that's our next step. Let's see what we can find out from the medical computers at least. Maybe his wife and kid got medical benefits over the years. It might give us an address."

"You know this is all illegal, right?" Ray felt obligated to point this out.

"He's dead. It might be a gray area," offered Sean.

"It's not a gray area and you know it."

"A man's gotta do what a man's gotta do. James' life is on the line. Let's just hope Sammy and his girlfriend feel the same way, if they believe us at all."

Chapter 13

It was Monday morning and Marybeth was driving into work. She had a standard routine on Mondays. Head to the shop. Drive around to the back and unload the weekend's purchases. Clean things up and price them, then enter them into the inventory. Well, technically, Angie did the inventory piece. Then Marybeth would go through the store and purge the shelves of old stock. Angie would take them out of the computer inventory and they would both load them back into Marybeth's car for her weekly visit to the woman's shelter. She'd been doing it for two years now and it had become familiar, automatic, normal, and this morning she needed normal. The only wild card was Angie.

Angie had been her assistant at the shop almost since the beginning two years ago. A single mom of three kids, she had started out at only a few hours a week. The schedule had slowly increased and now it was a few school hours a day on weekdays, and all day Saturday while Marybeth was yard saleing. They had gotten close over the years and Marybeth considered her a friend. Today, she had some explaining to do. Angie already knew something was afoot.

"Hey Angie," Marybeth greeted her as she walked through the back door to the shop.

"Good Morning, Angel," she said cheerily, using the nickname that the staff at the women's shelter had given her. "What happened this weekend?"

"Don't beat around the bush, Angie," Marybeth kidded. "And by all means, dispense with the pleasantries."

"Pleasantries are for people who don't know how to get to the point," she kidded back. "I have coffee and donut holes out front.

"Ah, a bribe," Marybeth observed.

"Yes, did it work?"

"Completely." They laughed and headed to the front of the store.

Grabbing their coffee and treats from the checkout counter, they took a seat on the sofa that had been sitting there for over a year. Items usually rotated out of the store long before one year, but this sofa seemed to belong right where it was, so Marybeth left well enough alone.

"So, what's going on and why is Josh in town early? Is everything okay with you two?"

"Completely," Marybeth assured her. "He came early for another reason altogether."

"Oh? Sounds mysterious." When Marybeth didn't respond immediately, she added cautiously, "It's not, is it? Mysterious?" Angie had been pulled into the drama of last year, having her own vision about her deceased sister that left her shaken for quite a while.

"Well, let's just say it's been an interesting weekend."

"Oh-oh. What does that mean exactly?"

"It has a flavor of last year around this time."

"You mean like Josh's dead mother hosting a bizarre yard sale?"

"Yes." Marybeth chuckled at the succinct summation. "Are you sure you want to hear it?"

Angie considered the questions for a moment. "Yes."

"Really? I expected you would want to stay as far away as possible after last year's revelations."

"Yeah, well, after I got used to whole idea of your new powers..."

"Wooaahh. Hold it right there," Marybeth interrupted. "I have no powers. None. These things are just ... (she searched for the word) circumstantial. That's all."

"Okay, sure," Angie acquiesced. "Call it whatever you want, but after I got used to the idea, it started to sound less demonic and more cool."

"Thanks for letting me off the demon hook."

"No problem. So, what happened?"

"Well, it was essentially the same, but the players are different." Marybeth was surprised how easily she talked about it. As if it was only slightly out of the ordinary. "It seems that Josh's mom was behind it but the yard sale *host* was a young soldier."

"Wow. What was he selling? Did you get those creepy visions?"

"There was a helmet and some love letters. And yes..."

"What did he want?"

Frustrated at Angie's constant interruptions, Marybeth held up her hands. "Angie, if you stop asking so many questions, I promise I'll tell you the whole story."

"Okay. Okay. Patience isn't my best thing. Maybe if I sit on my hands." She put her coffee down and shifted around on the sofa placing her hands, palms down, under her legs.

"Okay. So, here's what happened." Marybeth proceeded to recount the events of the yard sale and got almost all the way through before Angie was just about busting at the seams to ask questions.

"Wait." She took one hand out from under her leg. "Did you know him?"

"No. But it appears my father did."

"What?"

"First, put that away." Marybeth pointed at Angie's expressive appendage.

"Oh, yeah, sorry." Angie tucked her hand away to mirror its twin.

"So, I was saying..." and with that Marybeth was able to finish the story in between *oohs* and *aahs* and an occasional *What?* from Angie. When she was finished, she waited for the onslaught of questions that had been bubbling up.

"How can this guy not know where is son is? Don't ghosts know things like that?"

"I don't know. I'm not a ghost expert. But apparently not. The only thing we really have at this point is that his name was Bobby McMillan, and he had a wife and son, Rebecca and James. We don't even know if their last name is McMillan."

"That's not all you know," Angie pointed out. "You know that his son James was in the army and served in Iraq and Afghanistan. That's something. I have a couple of cousins that were in the army. They did tours over there too. They might be some help, at least with basic information. I can call them if you like. They live in Harrisburg. I haven't seen them in years but I'm sure they would want to help," she paused then added, "I think one of them, Joe, is a local cop now. I'm not sure where Jimmy's at. He might still be in."

Marybeth considered the offer. "I might take you up on that if nothing else shakes out. My dad is at the VA this morning trying to scare up a little more info. Let's wait and see what he finds, if anything."

"Okay, you'll let me know," Angie said. "Now, what's up for business today?"

They both turned their attention to the usual routine of the day, shifting items around and adding new inventory from Saturday's sales. Angie brought Marybeth up to speed on the events at the store over the weekend which was nothing out of the ordinary, especially relative to Marybeth's adventures. They were both unusually quiet, though, each reflecting on the story that was unfolding. While Marybeth worried about her dad, Angie started thinking about her own family, grateful that they had come home unharmed, as far as she knew anyway. She decided to call her mother later, just to check in and see how everyone was doing.

Chapter 14

Sean pulled up in front of the VA hospital like he'd done a thousand times before but today somehow it seemed different. He sat in his car thinking. There was an edginess to his nerves that smacked of the old PTSD days. Maybe he'd have to schedule an appointment to start therapy again, just to nip it in the bud, but not right now. Today he was meeting with two of the AVs. He mentally braced himself as he got out of the car and headed through the rotating door that lead to the lobby.

Ray was waiting for him inside. "Hey Sean. How're you doing?"

"Showing up."

"Did you get any sleep?" Ray noticed bags forming under Sean's eyes.

"Not much. But no nightmares. Just worrying a lot."

"Okay, that's something."

"I got a call from Marybeth this morning."

"Yeah? And?" Ray waited for a response.

"They found Bobby on the death tolls. His name is McMillan."

"Okay. Let's see where that gets us. You ready for this?"

"I have to be."

"I saw Sammy head in just before me, so I guess he's waiting for us at The Canteen."

"Let's do it."

They walked together down the long hallways of the hospital. It felt like a labyrinth getting to the cafe in the far back corner of the building. Usually it wouldn't have bothered Sean but today it seemed eerie, as if filled with the ghosts of soldiers wanting to tell their story. He listened for their voices but none came.

When they finally got to the small coffee shop, they spotted Sammy in the back at one of those ridiculously high pub-style tables. *Sniper Tables* Sammy called them, due to their vantage point over the standard tables that filled the middle of the room. Ray and Sean grabbed coffee at the counter and joined him.

"Good morning, Gentlemen," Sammy greeted them. "But apparently not for you Sean. You look like hell. What's up?"

"Good. I'd hate to feel this bad and people not know it." Sean tried for a little levity.

"Mission accomplished," Sammy bantered back. "What's going on?" He looked back and forth from Ray to Sean.

Ray lead in. "It's been a rough weekend for Sean. He pulled me in last night and we thought you might help out today."

"Okay. You got my attention."

"We need a favor," Ray went on. "We need your help in finding the family of a dead Vietnam Vet."

"You're kidding, right?"

"Nope," Ray nodded in Sean's direction. "But Sean has a story to tell you first."

"Christ. This is sounding worse all the time. Is this some old war story, 'cause I don't know if I'm up for it?" Sammy didn't like stories about combat, *Tales of Death* he called them.

Sean found his voice. "No. Nothing like that. Well, a little like that maybe, but not really."

"Just hear him out, Sammy."

"Alright. But I reserve the right to cut you off." Sammy didn't like talking about his time in country. He'd just as soon forget it ever happened and avoided rehashing old war stories. As far as he was concerned, it served no purpose except to bring people down.

"Understood." Sean nodded his head then looked down at his coffee. "Did anything strange ever happen to you over there, Sammy?"

They all knew what *over there* meant. "You mean besides being nineteen years old in a foreign country half way around the fuckin' world, in a jungle, shooting at people I never met for reasons I barely understood? Besides that?"

"Yeah. Besides that."

"No."

"Okay then. Try to keep an open mind." And with that, Sean launched into his story, past and present, trying to play down the more unusual aspects as quirky versus delusional. He wasn't having much success. When he was done, they all sat quietly for a moment.

"So, Sammy, what do you think?" ventured Sean.

Sammy sat there for moment. "I think my life is one long stay in a loony bin," he said as he rested his head in his hand.

"Yeah, well, welcome to my world," replied Sean. "So, will you help us out?"

"I can't actually do the helping. That has to be Sheila's call."

"Will you at least ask?"

"Yes. But I'm not telling her that whole story. I'll just say we need to get ahold of this guy's son because Sean has something to give him."

"You don't think she'd believe the truth?" Ray asked.

"I don't even know if I believe the truth," Sammy leaned in towards the other two, talking softly. "I know a lot of unbelievable things happened over there, so I don't doubt the story from Nam. But I'll admit that I'm having a hard time with how your daughter fits into things. That sounds a little far-fetched to me." Sammy thought a moment. "Do you think it's some kind of genetic thing with you and her and this spooky stuff?"

Sean didn't take offense at the *spooky* reference. He had been curious about it himself ever since Marybeth had shared her story. Were there other family members with any kind of special mojo? He had no idea. He had been distant from his parents for years, ever since he came back from Nam. Back then it had been his only way to cope but he knew it hurt them terribly. They had moved away brokenhearted. It was another guilt he had carried for years. He knew it was on him to break the silence, but as time went by it seemed harder and harder to bridge the gap. Every time he thought that maybe now was the time, he chickened out. Once again, he thought maybe now was the time.

"Sean? Hello?" Ray was waving his hands in front of Sean's face. "Where'd you go?"

"Nowhere you want to be," Sean replied putting these thoughts out of his mind.

Sammy was still a little skeptical. "What are you planning to do with the information if Sheila can get it?"

"I don't know exactly. Contact either one of them, I guess. I'm kinda making this up as I go. Is Sheila working today?"

"Yes, she is. So, I guess there's no time like the present." Sammy moved to get up. "Give me what ya got?"

Sean handed him a slip of paper with Bobby's full name, Robert McMillan, and below that was the date of death and serial number. Also listed on the page were his wife Rebecca and son, James, born 1969 or 1970 and recently retired from the Army.

"Well, that's quite a bit of information. Seems Sheila should be able to come up with something. Stay tuned," he said as he got up from the table. "I better not go in there empty handed though." He headed up to the coffee counter, ordered Sheila's favorite, then gave the other two a wave as he headed through the break in the railing that separated the cafe from the hospital's rear lobby.

"So now we wait," Ray pointed out, swigging his coffee.

"Yeah." Sean looked down, studying his coffee as if it were a crystal ball, looking for answers.

Sheila worked on the second floor in Billing. Sammy was fine-tuning the story he would tell her as he made his way to her office. She was usually busy, especially the week after bills were sent out and people were calling to complain or correct things. Rarely to pay. Thankfully, today was a calm day, in between the billing cycles.

"Hey Sheila," Sammy announced as he entered the office carrying a skinny mocha caramel coffee latte.

"Hey, Sam," she said, happily surprised to see him. Then her voice turned down a pitch. "What are you doing here? Are you okay?"

"I'm fine," he said, surprised at her reaction. "Why do you always think the worst?"

"Duh, this is a hospital. People come here when they're sick." She replied irritably.

"Oh, yeah. There's that. No, no. Nothing's wrong. I'm having coffee with Sean and Ray."

"Oh-oh. What kind of mischief are you guys cooking up now?" she kidded him.

"Well, funny you should ask." He placed the latte on her desk. "This is for you, from the guys." His smile had mischief written all over it.

"Uh huh. From the guys?"

"Yeah. To brighten your day."

"Uh huh. And what else?"

Sammy slid into the seat beside her desk that was usually reserved for customers. He lowered his voice and looked around for ease-droppers. Seeing no one nearby, he continued, "I know that what I'm going to ask you to do is a bit in the gray area."

She looked at him for a long moment. "Then it better have a good reason backing it up."

"Well, here's the thing. Sean was going through some old army stuff in his attic and he came across this helmet that he remembers doesn't belong to him. He switched helmets with some guy who ended up dead a few days later. Anyway, Sean wants to find this guy's son and give the helmet to him."

"So-o-o-o?" she said cautiously.

"So, Sean doesn't know where he is. He has this guy's name and serial number and we were wondering if you could tell us what his last known address was."

"From Vietnam?" Her voice raised a bit in annoyance.

"Shhhhhh." Sammy hushed her as he looked around for witnesses. "Yeah. From Vietnam."

"Honey, if you want those records you have to go two stories down into a basement in Texas and look through the boxes."

"Seriously?"

"Yeah. Hello? Pre-computer days."

"Oh, I almost forgot there was such a thing."

"Yeah. And no one is in a hurry to scan those things in. There's millions of them."

"Okay. How about this guy's son? He just retired from the Army maybe within the last month or so."

"Nope. This is the *Veterans* Administration. We don't have records for active duty soldiers, so unless he's checked into *this* VA, he's not in our system. And how do you know his son is retired military?"

"Okay, skip that part. Here's my last shot. This guy's wife's name is Rebecca McMillan if she hasn't remarried. Any chance you have something on her if she used the VA survivor medical benefits?"

"Now that I can work with. Let's see what I got." She tapped the serial number into the keyboard, scrolled through screens and tabbed past columns. "I got something here that says she is still using her medical benefits at this VA."

"Hot shit! Really?" Sammy almost popped out of his chair, then stealthily looked over both of his shoulders.

"Yeah. Really. But remember, you didn't hear it from me." Sheila was looking around now, too.

"Of course not. You got an address?"

"First, you all have to swear not to breathe a word of this."

"We swear. I swear, we all swear."

"Looks like she changed her name to Ross. 1142 Oakview Road, Harrisburg, PA. 555-683-2741."

Sammy scribbled the information down on his note paper, gave her a kiss on the forehead. "Sean owes you."

"I'll expect a day at the spa."

"You got it," he called as he headed back to the cafe.

He waved the piece of paper in the air as soon as Sean and Ray were in sight.

"I got it," he announced as he took his seat at the table.

"Really?" They both looked surprised.

"Yeah, really," Sammy said, hurt by their lack of faith.

"Okay, what exactly do you have?" Ray was skeptical.

Sammy resumed drinking his coffee in defiance, making them wait an extra moment for the info. Then puffed out his chest ever so slightly and tipped his chin up. "I got the address and phone number of Bobby's widow."

They all looked at each other, amazed, then started laughing and slapping Sammy on the back.

"Wow, that wasn't hard at all," said Sean.

"Maybe not for you," Sammy retorted, "but I had to pour on my lethal level of charm. I don't do it that often. It's very risky. We're lucky no one got hurt." He broke into a wide grin.

"And be assured we are eternally grateful to the Master." Ray held his hands up over his head and bowed up and down. They all knew Sammy had a way with the women.

"That's better. And you both owe Sheila a day at the spa."

"Done," they both agreed immediately.

"So, it seems like the hard part's done, then." Sammy shrugged.

"I'm thinking the hard part hasn't gotten here yet." Ray paused a moment, then nodded to Sammy. "Well, don't keep us in suspense. Where does she live?"

"Harrisburg."

"That's just down the road," Ray looked at Sean.

"Yeah, about an hour and a half or so, depending," Sean nodded.

"Yup," agreed Sammy. "So now what."

It was Sean who took over the conversation at this point. "I'll call her. Then if she lets me, I'll see her. I'll go by myself. I don't want to overwhelm her."

"Just a minute. You think you can cut us out of this story so easily?" asked Sammy, holding the slip of paper protectively close to his chest.

"Just for now. When I find out where James is, there will be plenty for all of us to do. I'll call her tonight. She might work during the day."

"Alright then. Are you going to be okay for the rest of the day?" Ray asked.

"If I'm not, I know who to call. Thanks guys." They all got up and walked back through the labyrinth together. Once in the parking lot, they parted company, heading to their respective cars.

As Sean drove home, he considered what he would say to Becky. How much would he share? He would have to ask about her son, of course. Does she know what kind of trouble he is in? Soldiers can hide things really well. He should know.

Chapter 15

It was a quiet afternoon at the shop and Angie's curiosity getting the best of her. Maybe she could help. If she talked to her cousins, maybe they would have some information or suggestions. They'd been in the military for years. They knew the system. She looked around to make sure the place was empty, picked up the phone and dialed her mother.

"Hi Mom. It's Angie. How's things going?"

"Good, honey. You know me. I'm keeping busy. How are things going with you?"

"Great, well, usually great, but I've been thinking lately..."

"Oh, no. That can't be good," Mom kidded.

"This is serious," Angie insisted.

"Okay, sorry." Mom's attitude shifted immediately. "What's on your mind? Are you okay?"

"Yes, Mom. I'm fine. It's not about me."

"What then?"

"Well, my boss has been talking about this friend of theirs. He's an Afghanistan Vet. And he's in trouble with some kind of post-traumatic stress and I started thinking about Joe and

Jimmy. I never hear anything bad, but I'm wondering if you know how they're doing."

"Oh, Angie. Everyone's okay, as far as I know, well, mostly, I guess."

"What does that mean?"

"Well, you know Joe is a cop now. He's been out for a few years. He's doing okay as far as I know, considering he puts his life on the line every day here in town. He brings a gun everywhere he goes, though, which is a little strange to me. Anyway, he seems to be doing fine. Now, Jimmy, he's a little bit of a different story."

"Is he still in the Army?"

"As a matter of fact, he just got out a few weeks ago."

"Really? Why haven't we had a welcome home party? He's home, isn't he?"

"Yes. He's home, but he specifically requested, demanded really, that there be no fanfare or parties celebrating his arrival."

"Why not?"

"Closest thing I can get from your aunt is that he's not feeling up to a lot of people jammed into the house and asking him a million questions."

"Since when is his family too much to handle?" Angie's volume was rising.

"I'm not sure, Angie, and I didn't pry."

"Pry? Why would you need to pry? Is there something they're not telling us? You think there's something wrong with Jimmy?" Distress was creeping into Angie's voice.

"Calm down, Angie. I don't know. Aunt Becky just said he's not himself. He gets angry a lot and yells at her and Uncle Mike. I imagine the stress of getting out of the Army after twenty plus years and coming home and acclimating into civilian life and looking for a job, all might be a little much. Don't you think?"

"I suppose so." She calmed down a little. "But now I'm a little worried. Are you going to be around this weekend?"

"I suppose so. Why?"

"Maybe I'll drop by and say hello. Maybe stop over at Jimmy's too."

"As you like. You know we always love to see you."

"It'll have to be Sunday. MB counts on me to keep the store open on Saturdays."

"Sure thing. You can call Jimmy when you get here. Maybe he'll want to see you."

"Alright, Mom. I'll see you this weekend. Love you."

"Love you too, dear. Bye."

Angie wandered around the shop for the next two hours, till closing time, ruminating over the conversation with her mom. What was going on? Something wasn't right. She could smell it. Whatever it was would have to wait for the weekend, a full six days away. She wasn't sure how she was going to make it that long.

Chapter 16

Sean sat in his kitchen for a long time, looking at his phone in one hand and the scrap of paper with Becky's information on it in the other. He had no idea how to even begin the conversation. Ultimately, he decided to wing it as best he could. He picked up the phone and dialed the number hoping it would be Becky who answered the phone.

"Hello?" came a woman's voice over the phone.

Sean's pulse quickened. "Hello. Is this Rebecca McMillan?"

The woman hesitated. "No, this is not." she said angrily. "This is Rebecca Ross. I have not been Rebecca McMillan for thirty-five years so if you are selling something or asking for money you had better get a new list and don't . . ..

"No. No. No," he interrupted her. He did not expect this at all. "Please wait. Don't hang up."

"What is it then?" she asked irritated.

"I'm sorry to bother you, Rebecca. I was a friend of your husband," he blurted out in a hurry hoping it would catch her attention and buy him another few seconds.

"What are you talking about *was*. You're not friends anymore? You can talk to him if you want. He's in the living room watching the news."

"No, Rebecca," he paused, "not that husband," was all Sean could think to say.

There was a long silence on the phone. "Oh." Becky could almost forget that she was married before. It was so long ago. But when something reminded her of it, she could still feel the ache in her heart. "You knew Bobby?" she said slowly. Then another long pause as she wondered what this call was about. "How?" she said abruptly, a bit of skepticism in her voice.

"I served with him in Vietnam. I was with him when he died." Sean knew it wasn't entirely true, but he needed something to get him in the door.

"Why are you calling me now? It's been forty years, Mr...?"

Sean realized he had not introduced himself, which he hurriedly corrected. "Sean. Sean Morgan."

Well, Mr. Morgan..."

"Please, call me Sean," he interrupted.

"Very well, Sean. Why now?"

"I've been going through my old army trunk and I have a few things that belonged to him. I thought maybe you might like them. Or maybe your son would. I think I remember he had a baby boy at home," he ventured into the subject of James.

"Like what? I can't imagine there's anything I want, but I guess Jimmy might be interested. He used to ask a lot about his dad but not for years."

"One of the things I have is Bobby's journal."

There was another pause on the phone. Then there was a voice in the background. A man's voice. "Is everything alright, Becks?"

108

"Yes, Mike. It's fine," she called back.

"Okay, Sean, you have gotten my interest, but I swear if this is some kind of scam you're running or you're looking for money or something, I'll have you arrested."

"No, ma'am. I swear. It's all on the up and up."

"I suppose you could mail it to me."

"I'm not that far away. I'm up in Pomroy, just outside of Philadelphia. I could drive down, if you like, and maybe tell you more about how I knew Bobby. That is, if you're interested."

Rebecca paused again. Did she really want to open up this wound? Even though it had been years ago, Bobby was still a part of her life. James had been a constant reminder, sometimes in a good way and sometimes not. James even looked like Bobby and had some of his mannerisms if that's even possible. At some point James might be interested in the conversation, but not now. He was fighting some inner battle that Rebecca couldn't help with.

"I suppose so. What do you suggest?"

"I can drive down and meet you anywhere you like. Bring James if he's around or your husband if it makes you feel better."

"Okay, but you can't come to my house."

"Fine, you name the place."

"There's a coffee shop-slash-bookstore nearby, Hot Topics Cafe, at the corner of Southbend Rd. and Walters St. I can give you directions."

"No need, ma'am. I'll find it. When?"

"Saturday, noontime."

"Nothing sooner?" Sean asked in a moment of panic.

"It's already waited forty years, Sean. Is there some reason it can't wait till Saturday?"

109

"No. No reason. I'll see you there."

When Sean hung up the phone his hands were trembling, and he had to take a minute to catch his breath. It didn't go as smoothly as he had imagined but she agreed to see him and that was the goal. If it had to wait till Saturday, then so it is. James will just have to hang on till then. And in the meantime, Sean had some catching up to do. He hadn't been paying too much attention to the current military conflicts. If he followed it too closely, he noticed his anxiety level start to increase a bit. There was no avoiding it completely though, and when the local news announced another native son coming home in a box, it sent Sean spinning into his own memories. He had managed to stay ahead of it over the years but staying ahead wasn't really dealing with it, just avoiding it. The strategy had worked so far but current circumstances were insisting on a new plan.

Chapter 17

Rebecca stood perfectly still, phone in her hand and tears in her eyes as the emotions washed over her. It was a familiar sadness. An indulgence, really, into the world of *what might have been.* She went there from time to time, in those intensely quiet moments. Not even quiet really, but still, like sitting in front of the Christmas tree on Christmas eve when everyone's asleep. Or when she gets home from work and, in the quiet of the house, she remembered it's the anniversary of her marriage to Bobby. At those moments the *what if* game played itself out in her imagination. It always played itself out perfectly of course. What's the sense of having a fantasy that ends badly? Then, after the fantasy, came the sadness, but it was worth it.

Her fantasy always came with a little guilt, too. After all, she'd been married to Mike now for almost thirty-five years. It had been a good life. Mike was a good man. A good husband and a good father for James, just like Bobby had asked her to do. Most days it didn't seem like there was ever anyone but Mike. He was the only father James had ever known. What was she doing, continuing to long for *what might have been?*

111

She started slipping back into the sadness when she was brought out of her trance by a voice from the living room. It was Mike. "Becks, you okay?"

Rebecca didn't answer, caught in her thoughts, unable, or unwilling to break free. Suddenly, Mike was at her elbow. "Honey, are you okay? Is something wrong?" She realized she was still standing there, frozen. The phone in her hand was beeping that off-the-hook alert of an inactive line.

"Yes. Yes, I'm fine."

Mike was not convinced. "Who was that?"

"He said he was a friend of Bobby's," she said as she slowly hung up the phone.

"Bobby? As in your first husband?" Mike asked surprised. He couldn't remember the last time his name had come up.

"Yes. He said he served with him in Vietnam. Said he was with him when he died."

"Seriously?" Mike was getting angry. "Is this some kind of a sick joke? A scam? Did he ask for money?"

"No. Nothing like that," she reassured him. "He said he has a few things that belonged to Bobby and that maybe I would want them."

"Do you believe him?" Mike had learned to trust Beck's intuition about people. She had a gift for sorting out the chaff from the grain, so to speak.

"I do, for now."

Mike turned Rebecca around and pulled her into his arms. She went easily, resting her head on his shoulder. He was a good man and Rebecca loved him dearly. But that first love lingered in her heart, an unrealistic measuring stick by which all other love pales. She tightened her hold on Mike as if hanging on to reality.

Mike tightened his arms around her in response, holding her close. He knew Bobby's ghost had been with them over the years. He didn't mind. He had never doubted Rebecca's love for him.

"Let's go sit down. I'll get you a glass of wine."

"Thanks." Rebecca allowed herself to be escorted to the living room.

Mike returned momentarily with two glasses of sparkling white zinfandel berry spritzer. Enjoying wine was getting almost as complicated as drinking coffee he noted as he handed the cold beverage to Rebecca.

"How are you feeling?" he asked.

She took a sip of wine and thought about it for a moment. "Like the past just hit me straight on at a hundred miles an hour and I couldn't get out of the way." Or was it that she didn't *want* to get out of the way.

"I can imagine that. It's quite a blast from the past. And we don't ever talk about it, really. Not even back then."

"Yeah. It was too painful back then and after a time it just seemed unnecessary. We got married and you became our family. And that was that." She took another sip.

"I don't ever talk about *my* experience either." Mike barely avoided the draft in 1970. "I had some good friends that died over there, too."

"I know you did. I remember you telling me about them."

"I think about them a lot. Every time there's a milestone in my life, I wonder what kind of life they would have led. The sadness never really goes away."

"You were lucky. Your number was never called. Bobby was drafted before they started that. Once you turned 18, they just sent you a letter telling you when to report."

"I *was* lucky. I knew it then and I know it now." He swirled his wine around in the glass. "I remember watching them pull the numbers on TV. I sat there all day waiting for my number. When it was called, 293, my mother cried."

"Did you?" she asked honestly.

"I sure wanted to. I was so scared and then so relieved to have a high number. But my dad was sitting right there too, and it didn't seem like the manly thing to do." He shrugged. "I was barely 18. Not even a man really." He sipped his fancy wine. "I can't tell you how painful it was to watch my friends all get called up.

"I remember those days. I had friends with lottery numbers too, but Bobby was already in by then, already overseas." Rebecca shifted in her chair. "There's still so much emotion about it. It's weird, after all these years."

"It was traumatic for the entire country, whether you went to war or not. And Vietnam came right on the heels of two other wars that left families in shock and grief."

"Yes, but those soldiers weren't drafted." Rebecca had a hint of resentment in her voice.

"They most certainly were." Mike countered, surprised she didn't know.

"What do you mean?"

"The US government started drafting men in 1942 and didn't stop until 1972."

"Really? Even during peacetime?"

"Yes. There were some volunteers, but not enough to adequately staff the needs of the military, even during peacetime. So, they drafted to fill in the difference."

"I always thought those conflicts were more *popular*, if you can say such thing about war. You know, people were more inclined to enlist on moral or patriotic grounds."

114

"They've all had their own supporters and detractors. The American people consistently said no to getting involved in World War II. They considered it Europe's war, until Pearl Harbor. And even then, there was opposition."

"Surely there was no pro Vietnam movement?" Rebecca was both fascinated and horrified by this information.

"Of course there was. A lot people saw communism as the rising up of the anti-Christ. They were completely in favor of sending troops wherever needed to stop the spread of evil. Others felt that if their government was asking them to fight, there must be a damn good reason. Even during the draft there were still a lot of people volunteering. All the women who served were volunteers."

"Oh, yeah. I never thought of that. What I remember of popular opinion doesn't seem to line up with the facts." Rebecca was starting to doubt her recollection of things. "How do you know all this stuff anyway?"

"Partly, I lived it. Partly, I was a political science major in college."

"Oh no! You didn't occupy any of the administration buildings, did you? Wow! We never really *have* talked about this, have we?"

"I never wanted to be disrespectful to Bobby's memory." Mike dodged the question.

"Oh my God, you did! Please tell me you were never outside the main gate of Fort Devens."

"No. I was never that bold, but I did show up at a few local *discussions*."

"Oh, is that what you were calling them?" Rebecca didn't know why but she was starting to get defensive.

Mike was feeling bad about how this was going. "If this is upsetting you, I'm sorry. Let's talk about something else."

115

"No. No, it's alright." Rebecca backed down. "I guess this is why we never talked about it."

"Yeah. And as you pointed out, it's still a very emotional topic."

"I'd like to keep talking about it but maybe in smaller chunks. And maybe let's wait for this *friend of Bobby* thing to blow over."

"Agreed."

Chapter 18

S ean had a fitful night's sleep filled with nightmares and memories of things he had hoped he'd forgotten. He woke up in a sweat, heart thumping in his chest. It was a little after 4 AM and it was the third time he'd woken up that night. He decided to get up instead of stressing about going back to sleep and having another nightmare. It hadn't been this bad in a lot of years. He was hoping it would pass.

He wandered into the kitchen and turned on the coffee pot. He had set it up the night before just like he always did so he wouldn't have to mess with it in the morning. He heard the pot crackle to life and the smell of the dark elixir soon filled the air. It was a soothing aroma and it eased his nerves even before the first sip passed his lips. He didn't wait for the pot to stop brewing. He pulled the carafe out, poured himself a cup and sat down at the kitchen table. His tremors finally began to calm down as his brain came online.

He thought about having a drink, but he knew he wouldn't. It was just an old strategy he'd used in the past that didn't work. He thought about calling Ray, but he knew he wouldn't do that either. He reserved 4 AM calls for life or death situations and this was not one of them. He thought back to those early days when he had first started having the PTSD symptoms. He had no idea what was happening to him. There was constant worrying that tipped over into paranoia on occasion. And the physical jumpiness felt as if every nerve in his body was on high alert. The slightest unexpected noise would send an electric current from head to toe resulting in muscle tension and heart palpitations. But the worst for him was the hopelessness that settled in. He would isolate himself in the house with a hundred different emotions taking turns battering his psyche. He knew why people killed themselves. He had been to that edge himself more than once. He never really wanted to die. He just wanted the pain to stop.

He recognized the symptoms now, not that it was much help. When the symptoms came on, they had a life of their own. His rational brain was trained to help mediate the mental mess by a practice called mindfulness, noticing your immediate surroundings, calling them out loud. He consciously reminded himself where he was and what the date was. He told himself that he was safe and the noises of the night were just the creaks of an old house and nothing more. This was a mind game and he knew how to play it now, with skills acquired through therapy. Time had assisted him in healing some of the old wounds. Maybe current events would heal the rest.

Chapter 19

Marybeth scrapped her usual Saturday plans of rotating through the yard sale/flea market circuit to accompany her dad on the hour and a half drive to Harrisburg. Dad was concerned that Rebecca might feel overwhelmed by more than just himself, but Marybeth argued that having his daughter at his side might lend him some legitimacy and offer Rebecca a sense of safety. He relented under the pressure. Having her along meant Josh too, of course. And there was no talking Ray out of it. So, this morning the four of them were gathered outside his house for the road trip. He was in possession of the helmet in a plastic shopping bag tucked under his arm. Marybeth had the love letters and journal along with the necklace tucked into a decorative pouch she purchased from the stationary story in town, acid-free for archival material, to keep them safe. The pouch was then snuggled in her generously sized purse that she sometimes referred to as the *Bottomless Pit*.

"I still don't like this. If Rebecca sees all of us lying in wait, it might just spook her, and we'll be scrambling around for a

Plan B." Sean was wringing his hands and pacing in the driveway.

Ray reassured him for the fifth time. "Look, Sean. First, we don't have any idea how this is going to go. For all we know, James will show up and things will go sideways fast. You'll need us there for that." Ray waited for Sean's response.

"Okay. I get that. What's the second thing?"

"What do you mean?"

"You said *first*, implying there is a second."

"Oh, I don't know. That was the important one. Anyway, Josh and I will be at a different table. She won't even know we're with you. So please stop going over this."

"Right," Sean relented. "Let's just get this over with."

"Let's go then." Ray pushed the button on his key ring and the door locks on his Chevy Tahoe released with a recognizable click. Marybeth and Josh took the back seats as Sean and Ray loaded themselves into the front. They were all silent as Ray pulled out of the driveway and headed toward the interstate.

The ride to Harrisburg was a quiet one. Sean turned the helmet over absentmindedly, wishing he could talk to Bobby again, even for a moment, and get a little guidance but the ether was silent.

As they got closer, they began to strategize about the meeting. How much would they tell her? How much would she believe? Josh and Sean preferred the tell-all approach while Marybeth and Ray preferred a need-to-know plan. In the end, they agreed to play it by ear, but that Sean had the lead.

A few minutes later, they walked into the Hot Topics Cafe. Marybeth and Sean found a table in the corner with a view of the door, hoping for at least the minimum of privacy. Josh and

Ray took up a position at a neighboring table with a clear line of sight. Marybeth was the first to spot Rebecca as she walked in. She looked remarkably like the woman in her vision even after all these years.

"There she is," she said in a hushed tone, grabbing Dad's arm.

"Are you sure?"

"Yes, I'm sure," she said irritably.

"Okay. Okay. Here we go." Sean stood up at the table, getting her attention. She assumed this was the man on the phone and walked slowly in his direction.

Sean extended his hand. "Hi. Are you Rebecca?"

"Yes." Rebecca accepted his handshake.

"I'm Sean. We spoke on the phone."

"Yes. Hello. Nice to meet you."

"I have my daughter with me. I hope you don't mind."

Marybeth stood and repeated her father's greeting with a handshake introduction.

"Hi. I'm Marybeth, Sean's daughter."

"Hello. Nice to meet you." Rebecca took a seat. "I must admit, I'm a little nervous *and* a little skeptical."

"I don't blame you," Sean reassured her. "I thought maybe you'd bring your husband with you."

"No. I decided if this was the real deal, I'd rather deal with it alone initially."

The waitress came over and they all ordered coffee.

"I understand," Sean continued. "Would you like to ask us a few questions or would you rather we offered a little more information?" Sean was doing his best to pace himself and not overwhelm her with information.

"I don't know what to think. It's been so many years and life goes on. But since we talked, I've been remembering all kinds of things. It's makes me a little sad, really."

It was Marybeth who jumped in. "We're sorry if we have cause you any pain. We were hoping it would mean a little closure for you and your son. I understand that you're a bit skeptical. How did your son handle the news?"

Rebecca hesitated. "I didn't say anything yet. Jim's in a hard place right now."

"I'm sorry," Marybeth went on. "Is he ill?"

"That's part of it. He just got back from serving in Afghanistan."

"Ah, a soldier like his dad," Sean chimed in. "It must be good to have him home. Considering your prior experience, you must have been a wreck the whole time he was gone."

Rebecca started to look a little suspicious at the inquiry about James. "This is about Bobby though, right?"

"Yes. Yes, of course." Sean pulled the helmet out of the bag he'd been holding on his lap. "As I said on the phone, I was with Bobby in the end. This here is his serial number. 52-462-"

"-893." Rebecca finished the numbers from memory. When Sean looked at her curiously, she added, "I used those numbers for years accessing survivor benefits."

"Right." Sean nodded. "Of course."

Rebecca took the helmet from him and turned it over in her hands. Marybeth and Sean stiffened slightly and looked at each other, wondering if anything unusual would happen. If so, Rebecca didn't let on. She wasn't crying exactly but a profound sadness seemed to come over her. They all sat uncomfortably with the silence, waiting for Rebecca to make the next move.

Rebecca finally spoke. "Why are you here Sean? And don't tell me it's just to return a stinky old combat helmet from forty years ago."

The question caught Sean off guard. Reverting to the truth, he answered her as calmly as he could.

"I have reason to believe that your son James is in trouble."

Again, there was a long silence as Rebecca's stare bore right through him.

"And why would you think that?" Protective mama bear was out of the cave.

It was Marybeth who offered the next answer. "My dad and I have a way of knowing things that most people, including us, don't really understand." She paused for a moment before she went on. "Bobby got a message to us that James might need some help."

Rebecca sat up straight. "Really?" Hostility was creeping in to the conversation. "Voices from the grave told you to call me? And help my son? What kind of a scam are you running because it's cruel and will get you nowhere with me?"

"It's not a scam Rebecca. Really." Sean was almost pleading.

"Well, apparently this is his helmet but the rest of it all smells a lot like bull crap to me. So, I'll be taking this with me. Don't call me again."

Josh was watching the conversation just out of earshot, but he knew it was going badly. He saw Rebecca's aura go flaming red and flash out around her body.

"No. Rebecca, please wait," Sean tried to turn it around. "It's the truth. Really."

"Leave me alone," Rebecca shot back as she headed for the door.

Marybeth put her hand on Dad's arm just as he was getting up to follow her.

"Don't Dad. She's upset. Let her be. I can't say I blame her."

"But what about James?" Sean ran his fingers through his hair.

"I don't know. We'll think of something."

Just then, Josh and Ray appeared at the table.

"What happened?"

"It looks like we spooked her off." Sean pounded his fist on the table garnering curious looks from nearby patrons.

"You hit a nerve for sure, Sean. She turned flaming red just before she left. It usually means fear."

"What are you talking about? You couldn't even see her from over there," Sean countered. Ray shot Josh a sideways glance as well.

Marybeth and Josh exchanged a look. "Josh sometimes puts color to things, you know, to help him think. We can explain it later."

"Yeah, right." Sean seemed to blow it off.

Ray continued to stare at Josh for another moment then turned to Sean. "Okay. It's all good." Ray calmed him down. "We'll just switch up to Plan B."

"There is no Plan B." Sean forced the words through gritted teeth.

"Hey." Ray looked him straight in the eye. "Then let's go make one."

Sean took a deep breath. "Yeah, you're right. And let's do it fast. I have a bad feeling about this."

Josh chimed in with his voice of reason. "Let's get out of here and head home. We can brain storm in the car and then get dinner back in Pomroy."

They agreed and headed out to the car.

Marybeth pulled Josh just far enough behind to whisper, "What are you doing? They don't know about you."

"You mean about auras?" Josh whispered back, offended.

"Yes! This is already complicated enough."

"I understand that. But, considering the stories that have been told over the past few days, don't you think it's worth sharing? Especially if I can add some information to the mix?"

Marybeth was silent.

"Oh. So that's how it is. You're embarrassed or ashamed or you don't believe me. Which is it?"

"It's not like that."

"Oh, it's not?"

"Can we talk about this later?" She whispered even lower as they approached the other two at the car.

"Count on it." He whispered back.

"Are you two okay?" Sean asked. "There's a lot of whispering going on."

"We're fine Dad. We'll explain later."

Chapter 20

Rebecca was trembling with emotions she couldn't identify as she rushed out of the restaurant. She collapsed into her car and then sat quietly, holding the helmet to her chest, trying to calm down. What was she so upset about? This conversation had been exactly what she expected. Some guy had Bobby's helmet and wanted to give it to her. That's pretty much what happened so what was the problem? The conversation had turned to Jim. That was the problem. She was concerned about him, but she wasn't ready to share her fears, and certainly not with total strangers. After all, Jimmy's business was his own, wasn't it? She knew his current state didn't truly represent who he was and she didn't want strangers making assumptions based on his recent erratic behavior. She was hoping it would pass.

She said a prayer for him before she left the parking lot. Her church prayer group was doing the same. She had to have faith. Her daughter-in-law and grandchildren needed him. Technically it was her ex-daughter-in-law, but she never looked at it that way. "What God has brought together, let no man put asunder." How long had Jim's behavior been off? She wondered if that was part of the split-up. Right now, she just had to get home. She turned on the ignition and pulled out of the parking lot.

She dropped the helmet on the kitchen table a little harder than she intended. The resultant bang brought Mike around the corner into the kitchen instantly.

He had been waiting in the den for her return but didn't want to accost her as soon as she walked in the door. He jumped up at the noise. When he got to the kitchen, Rebecca was flushed and breathing hard.

"Beck. What's up? What happened? I knew I should have gone with you." He reached out to hug her, but she shook him off.

"I'm fine. Those two just got my blood boiling a bit."

"Two? I thought you were only meeting Sean? What happened?" Concern and then anger crept into his voice. "Was this a scam? Did they try to get money from you?"

"No. It wasn't that. But there was definitely something they weren't telling me."

"Who is *they*?" he insisted.

"She said she was his daughter. She looked about right so I guess that's true."

"So, *what happened*?" Mike overemphasized the question.

"It started out okay. Sean showed me the helmet with Bobby's serial number, so I assume it's his but then the conversation turned, and they were asking lots of questions about Jim."

"Like what?"

Just then Jim rounded the corner from the den where he was watching TV and drinking beer. "Yeah. Like what?" He had his now usual irritated edge.

"Oh, it's nothing." Rebecca tried to backtrack.

"No. It's not. Who's asking about me. And what's that?" He pointed to the helmet.

"Really Jim. It's nothing. Please don't worry about it."

"Ma, it's obviously something. Stop treating me like a child." His tone was inching its way up.

Rebecca hesitated. "I got a call last week from someone claiming to be a friend of your dad's."

Jim looked at Mike. "Yeah? So?"

"Not Mike." Rebecca let that sink in a moment. "Bobby."

There was a long silence as Jim processed this information. His body twisted and tensed as a hundred emotions fought their way to the surface.

Rebecca went on quickly hoping to defuse the situation. "He gave me that helmet. He said it was Bobby's and that he had letters too, but I got a sense something wasn't right, so told him to get lost."

"And he was asking about me?"

"Apparently Bobby told him he had a son named James."

"And what did this guy want?" The words were pushed through clenched teeth.

"Jimmy, really, don't make a big deal out of this. I don't know what he wanted, but I told him to get lost."

Jim was holding tightly to the back of the kitchen chair in an effort to stay the wave of emotions. It was getting harder and harder to maintain any kind of self-control and he often felt like he was at the mercy of some crazed version of himself.

"Why now!" Jim demanded. But the question was not to Rebecca or Mike. It was to the air, to the unseen presence of Bobby. "Why are you fucking with me!" Jim slammed his hand on the chair. "I can't fucking take this right now!" Jim looked around for his coat.

"Jim, calm down. Really. This is nothing. Go sit in the living room. I'll make us lunch."

"Food doesn't fix everything, Mom!" He grabbed his jacket off the hooks by the door.

"Jim. Please don't go off like this. I'm worried." Rebecca was pleading now. Jim looked for his car keys.

Mike took his turn. "Jim. Calm down. You're upsetting your mother."

Jim's temper was still on the rise. "All the more reason for me to get out of here. That's all I do lately is upset people." He located his keys and headed for the door.

"Jim! Please don't go out like this." Rebecca was near tears.

Without another word, Jim slammed the door behind him. They watched as he got into his truck and squealed out of the drive.

Rebecca collapsed into a chair in tears. "I don't know how much longer I can take this, Mike. Maybe Sean and his daughter are right. Maybe they *can* help."

"I don't know, but why don't you back up and tell me everything."

On the highway back to Pomroy, the team deconstructed the meeting, looking for any possible positive spin.

Marybeth was empathizing with Rebecca. "I don't think it went that badly. She just has to let it sink in. It's overwhelming."

"Maybe so," Sean agreed, "but if she can't get past her denial that there's a problem, her son pays the price."

Marybeth countered, "In all fairness, we've never met James and for all we know there isn't a problem."

"So, you think a ghost comes back from the dead for nothing?" Sean was getting heated.

So was Marybeth. "Well, for a dead person he didn't seem to have a lot of other information, did he?"

"Oh, taking pot shots at a fallen soldier now because he doesn't have the answers you want?"

Ray finally spoke up. "Look, this is getting nowhere. Can you two refocus please?"

Still irritated, Sean went on, "And what was that 'turning red' all about Josh?"

Josh was a little caught off guard by the turn in conversation. He hesitated. "I guess you need to ask your daughter." He turned to Marybeth, refusing to say more.

All eyes focused on Marybeth. "What do you mean ask me?" she said defensively.

"Apparently, I'm not allowed to talk about it. And, apparently, you haven't said anything to your dad about it. So, how do you want to play that?"

"It's not like that," Marybeth squirmed.

"What's it like then?" Josh was not letting her off the hook.

Marybeth quieted down. She looked at Josh affectionately. "It's really not like that. There never seemed to be an opening to bring it up. That's all. Really." She reached out and took his hand.

"Now's a good time," he replied, looking back into her eyes.

"Helloooo? A good time for what?" Sean was losing his patience again.

"Josh has his own unique ability, sort of like what we're talking about here, but different. He sees auric fields."

Ray and Sean looked at each other, then returned their gaze to the road. There was a moment of silence in the car, while Ray and Sean waited for an explanation.

After an awkward moment, Marybeth prompted Josh with a wave of her hand. "Ah, Josh?"

He waited another couple of second in defiance and then explained. "Auric fields are energy fields that surround all living things and, in some cases, not living or previously living, similar to the idea of halos. The colors change based on the frequency and intensity of what's happening emotionally."

"And you see these things all the time?" Sean was curious.

"Most of the time, but I've learned to tune them out so now sometimes I have to consciously look for them."

"And, Marybeth, you didn't think this would be helpful information?" Sean was cross again.

"I'm sorry. Alright? It just didn't occur to me to share Josh's information or it didn't seem like the right time. We're here now. Can we move forward please?"

Ray looked into the rear-view mirror at Josh in the back seat. "So, what about the red?"

"I saw fiery flashes of red spiking out of Rebecca this morning. It usually means that someone is quickly and fiercely angry or afraid. I don't exactly interpret them much beyond the context of the situation. I didn't hear the conversation, so I can't say much more about it."

"She left when Dad asked her about James."

"Oh, then I would guess she's protecting him for some reason, fiercely, like a primitive instinct."

"So not really in denial," Sean mused, "just doesn't want anyone to know how bad it is."

"Yeah, Dad. I can appreciate that. I hope you would do that for me?"

"Probably not. For your sister maybe." Sean grinned.

Marybeth reached through the bucket seats and punched her dad on the shoulder. "Not funny."

Ray gave a chuckle. "Alright then. Now can we get back to business?"

They spent the rest of the drive considering ideas about their next move and supposing a lot about what might be going on. By the end of the day the best plan they could come up with was to return to Harrisburg tomorrow, this time to Rebecca's house, and risk being arrested for trespassing. James' life was on the line and they had to do whatever it took to get through.

Chapter 21

Josh and Marybeth had hardly gotten through the kitchen door when Josh opened the hostilities. "So, now maybe we have the time to talk about us."

"Us? What do you mean us? What are you talking about?" Marybeth was squirming.

"MB, we've been seeing each other for a year now without ever actually talking about our relationship because every time I bring it up, you dodge the conversation somehow." Josh's temper was high, and this whole *I don't know what you're talking about* game was old.

"Not true." Marybeth attempted a defensive move.

"Yes, it is true," he insisted. He pulled off his coat and hung it on the back of the kitchen chair.

"I just don't feel like we have anything to talk about. What's to say?" She slammed her pocketbook down on the table.

"Really, MB? That's the best you can do? After a year?"

"What do you want me to say? Things are going fine, aren't they?" She yanked her coat off and hung it roughly on the hook by the door.

135

"Sure. Except that you're embarrassed by who I am and how I see the world."

"What are you talking about?"

"You know damn well what I'm talking about and if you don't, then maybe you're right. We don't have anything to say." Josh could feel his temper rise and his heart break simultaneously.

Marybeth hesitated a moment too long.

"Okay, then. I'm done getting pushed away. This will be my last visit here."

"What are you talking about?" She was shocked.

"If you don't have anything to say, then neither do I." He stood perfectly still, staring her down.

"Is all this about this afternoon?" she yelled back at him. "I'm sorry! Alright?"

"That's a terrific apology, MB! Could you have put any less thought into it? Come on, one more time, with meaning."

She had never seen him so out of sorts. They had had a few arguments on the phone and there had been a few days of radio silence on occasion, but they always seemed to work it out.

"Look, we've had disagreements before. Let's just talk it out," she tried to reason.

"Okay. Start talking."

"I'm sorry about this afternoon, about not saying anything to my dad about your sight."

"Is that what you think this is about?"

"I don't know, Josh. And I feel like I need to know, and I need to know now. You know I'm not a deep thinker. You're the one who analyzes everything."

"MB, it's our anniversary and you are blowing it off like it's nothing. And now there's a huge crisis going on and you won't let me in! You won't let me help. You didn't even want to tell your father that I have something to contribute! Really? I might as well go home."

"That's not true. You've been helping...a lot. You've been taking care of me." Marybeth's voice got a little quieter as she calmed down. "That's how you help."

"Great, but I'm a part of this, MB, not some outsider. And you don't include me in things. So, what's going on?" Josh was lowering his voice too.

"I don't know."

"Bullshit."

"I don't know how to say it. You're better at words than I am."

"Okay, how's this. We've been getting together now for almost a year, just you and me, in our little bubble, cherishing our time together and, as a result, not including each other in our lives. I think I've done better than you but I'm not without fault. I try to make time to see my family when you come up, but when I come down here, we don't do anything with anyone, not family, not friends. I'm not part of your life in any way."

"I guess I never looked at it that way."

"And whenever I try to talk to you about it, you blow me off. And don't say you don't."

"Okay. It's hard for me to talk. Period. Especially about things that are important to me. It's not that I don't listen to you. I do. And I do think about what you say. I just don't see any point in talking about it."

"Well, I do."

"Yeah, I'm getting that."

"So, what is so hard about talking about us?" They had settled down enough for cautious conversation.

"Well, first of all, I don't think about things as much as you do. I just don't. And when I do, I get worried and confused. You say a year like it's a long time. I think a year doesn't even scratch the surface. Eric and I knew each other a year before we got married. Look what a colossal mistake that was. You knew Jan for less than that when you moved in together. Look how that ended." She took a deep breath and waited.

"This is nothing like Jan for me. Is this like Eric for you?"

"Well, no. Of course not."

"Then why are you comparing us to that?"

"Because it's the only measuring stick I have." Marybeth was close to tears.

"Then let's create another measuring stick. One that's just for us."

"I don't know how."

"I don't know either but let's figure it out together."

"I'm sorry. I'm sorry." She was weeping now.

Josh was tearing up a little too.

"I'm sorry too." He reached out for her and she easily slipped into his embrace. They stayed that way for a long time.

"MB," Josh started again, still holding her close. "Sometimes I feel like I'm dragging you into this relationship against your will. Like there's a constant push-back from you."

"I know. I'm afraid."

"And I'm tired. I can't be both halves of this relationship."

"I don't know how to not be afraid."

"If you're not looking for any more than what we currently have, a weekend every few weeks, then we need to have a different conversation."

"What are you saying?"

"I'm saying that you need to get in or get out."

138

She held onto him tighter. He responded in kind. He didn't want it to be over either, but he didn't see any future in the status quo. He wanted more.

"Let's talk about it later," Marybeth mumbled into his shoulder.

"That's what you always say."

She pulled back just enough to look him in the eyes. "This time I mean it." He knew she meant it in that moment, but he was skeptical of her resolve.

She sank deeper into his embrace. "But right now, I'm exhausted."

"Me too," he said, kissing the top of her head.

Chapter 22

As agreed, they had all met at Sean's for the next attempt to save a man they'd never met. Their first stop was Marybeth's shop to let Angie know she'd be on her own today. The guys waited for her in the car out front.

"Hey, MB." Angie looked up from polishing a silver platter when she heard the door open. She was dressed in her usual chaos of colors and big jewelry.

"Hey, Angie. How's it going?"

"Great, MB. How's the soldier mystery going? I've been dying to hear." She put down the polish to give Marybeth her full attention.

"Well, now that you've asked...I need to take the day off today. Are you okay with the store?"

"Sure. What's up?"

"We met with James' mother yesterday and it was close to a disaster. I don't know what we're going to do now except we're going back today to try again."

"Wow. Wait a minute. You mean, since Monday, you got an address and phone number *and* set up a meeting? That's amazing. How did you do all that?"

"My dad got the info from the VA and then told me not to ask any more questions. So, I didn't."

"Gotcha. Well, what happened? What went wrong?"

"We were meeting with Rebecca and she started getting suspicious. I can't blame her. She was asking questions about why we were *really* there. Then Dad blurted out that we got this message from Bobby." Marybeth waved her hand toward the sky and looked up, "and that pushed her over the edge. She told us to leave her alone and stormed out of cafe. It wasn't good."

"So, you're going back today? Are you sure that's a good idea?"

"No. But we couldn't think of anything else. Maybe James will be there or maybe we could talk to Rebecca's husband and have more luck."

"Well, that's pretty bold. They could have you arrested you know."

"Yeah. We already considered that."

"Where do these people live?"

"Harrisburg."

"Really? That's where I'm from. My family's all there."

"We met at a place called Hot Topics. It's a..." Marybeth didn't get a chance to finish before Angie interrupted.

"It's a cafe and book store. I know exactly where that is. I love that place."

"Yeah, well, I wish I could have enjoyed it more, but we were in and out in pretty short order."

"Where do they live? Wouldn't it be a hoot if I knew them?"

"Nothing surprises me anymore," Marybeth mumbled under her breath. She pulled a piece of paper out of her pocket and read off the address. "Their name is Ross at 1142..."

"Oakview Road!" Angie shouted.

"Yeah." Marybeth stared back at her. "How do you know?"

Angie's eyes got as big as saucers, as a dawning awareness came over her.

"Rebecca and Mike Ross?" she asked almost in a whisper, forcing the air out of her lungs.

"Yeah," Marybeth said again. "You know these people Angie?" Marybeth couldn't believe it.

"It's my Aunt Becky and my cousins." Angie was barely breathing.

"What? The one who has the two sons who are veterans?"

"Yeah." Angie plopped herself down on the couch. "I just called my mom the other day and she said my cousin Jimmy just got out and is having a hard time. Are you saying that cousin Jimmy is this guy's son? How is that possible?" Angie was starting to panic. "MB, is Jimmy going to kill himself!" she shouted, popping out of her seat at the realization.

Marybeth was getting caught up in Angie's panic. "I don't know! I don't even know if it's the same family but it sure sounds like it is."

"Oh my God, oh my God, oh my God! This can NOT happen! AGAIN!" Angie's brain went screaming back to memories of her sister Jackie who killed herself six years earlier. She started hyperventilating.

"MB, I can't do this again. I can't. I can't. I can't."

Marybeth grabbed her by the shoulders and shook her. "Angie. Angie. Get a hold of yourself."

The guys were watching the exchange through the boutique's large storefront windows. Sean and Josh both made a move towards the door.

143

"I've got this." Sean waved Josh back as he jumped out of the car. Josh got out as well, but remained behind, at the ready, should things get worse.

He raced into the store catching both Marybeth and Angie by surprise. "Hey. What's going on here? Angie, are you okay?"

Both Marybeth and Angie started talking at once.

"Whoa. Okay. One at a time. Marybeth, what's up?"

"It seems that the soldier we are looking for is also Angie's cousin, Jimmy. She mentioned him the other day, but we didn't put things together till just now. And..."

Sean put up a hand to stop her. "Okay. Angie? How do you know this?"

"After MB told me your story, I got to thinking about my family, so I gave my mother a call this week. She said my cousin, Jimmy, just got home a few weeks ago and was not doing well, isolating in his room and getting angry at my Aunt Becky. Sean, if he's going to kill himself, I have to get there now, like yesterday." Angie started looking around furiously for her purse and keys. Acquiring both, she headed for the door.

"Okay. Hold up." Sean moved strategically in front of the door. "I'm not sure what I missed here but if you go running off to Harrisburg, you'll spook him, and he'll take off. Then no one will be able to talk to him."

"I won't spook him. He knows me. We grew up together."

"I know you think that. But I'm telling you, we're dealing with PTSD here. I know what I'm talking about." Sean was feeling his own panic rise.

"He knows what he's talking about Angie. He's been through it. You gotta listen to him." Marybeth was trying to be reassuring but it only agitated Angie all the more.

"What are you saying? I should do nothing? Oh no. Been there. Done that. Not doing it again." It was a flat-out statement of fact.

Sean had no idea what she was talking about, but he didn't have time to deter from the task at hand for even a moment. "Okay, Angie. I get it. Let's just take one minute and think how you can help."

"Help you? You don't even have a plan. You're just going to go barging in and hope for the best."

"Well," Sean hedged, "not entirely true but not wrong either. We can't really have a plan until we know the lay of the land and we can't know that until we talk to Rebecca."

"Okay, then, let's go. It will work out perfectly because she'll be more inclined to believe your bizarre story if I'm there backing you up."

"It's a great idea, Angie, but we can't go in there in a panic. It will not help anyone."

Marybeth had reached out to take her hand in an effort to calm her down. It worked.

"MB, what if he does something before we can talk to him?" Angie was almost in tears.

"We'll get there in time, Angie. I know we will," she reassured her.

"Angie," Sean's voice was calming and confident, "We need to stay calm and we need to get to your Aunt Becky's."

Angie took a deep breath. "Okay, but can we leave now?"

"Yes. The car's out front, gassed up and ready to go."

Chapter 23

Angie slid into the back seat after Marybeth, who was now middle man. Once in the car, Angie took out her cell phone and called her mother. She put it on speaker phone.

"Hey Mom. I have a weird question. Well, it might not be weird. I guess it depends on the answer but it..."

"Angie. Ask me the question already."

"Is Mike Jimmy's father? Like real father?"

"Why would you ask such a question?"

"Okay, so that's not an answer. So, I'm guessing he's not."

"Well, he certainly is by any definition you chose to use," her mom said defensively.

"Okay, I use the sperm donor definition."

"Angie! There's no need to be crude."

"Answer the question, Mom. It's really important."

"Well, in that context, no."

"No? How is that possible?"

"In the usual way, I guess."

"No. How is it possible that I don't know that!"

"That all happened before you were born, Angie. Aunt Becky never wanted to talk about it and I guess we all just

147

moved on. She married Uncle Mike and that was that. What is this about?"

"Who is Jimmy dad?"

"Angie, really, why are you so upset?"

"Please just tell me."

"Jimmy's dad died in Vietnam when he was a baby." The statement seemed to suck all the air out of Angie's lungs. "Becky remarried before James' second birthday. He adopted James and then they had Joey. Honestly, I don't ever even think about it anymore."

Angie went on in a flat tone. "What was his name, Mom?"

"Bob. Bob something. I don't remember the last name, Angie, honestly, I don't. Now please tell me what's going on. You're worrying me."

"I can't say right now, Mom, but I promise I'll tell you everything later."

"Are you in some kind of trouble?"

"No Mom. I promise. I'll call you later." Angie hung up before the conversation could go on.

She looked up and all eyes were on her, including Ray's in the rear-view mirror alternating back and forth to the road.

"Okay Angie." It was Sean who got down to business. "Tell us what you can about James."

"Well, I don't know what to say. We were close as kids, but he's been away a lot since he joined the Army. I don't know him that well as a grown up."

"Tell us what you know."

"Okay. We were close as kids even though he was older than me. He was your normal nice kid, played sports, you know, the usual things." Angie tried not to get lost in her memories. "He graduated from high school and joined the Army. He got married then got divorced. Oh, and had two kids in between there. And that's pretty much what I know. And he has been over to both Iraq and Afghanistan several times."

"Where are is ex-wife and kids."

"They were somewhere in Maryland last I knew. Near DC I think."

"How old are they?" Marybeth chirped in. "And what are their names."

"Oh, God. I don't know. I only see them at holidays. Todd is maybe ten or so and little Chrissy, well, not so little anymore, is two years younger so maybe eight-ish. Why?"

Sean explained, "The more personal information we have about him the more we can engage him in conversation."

Ray took over, "The longer we can keep him in conversation, the longer we can keep him alive."

"Oh my God." Angie put her head in her hands and started to hyperventilate.

The remainder of the ride was mostly silent broken by a few questions here and there as everyone sorted the information out in their own heads. Then the GPS gave up its last direction.

"*You will reach your destination in two miles.*"

"Okay everyone. Listen up." It was Ray who took charge now. "I've been thinking about our next move. We're almost there. We need a plan. Here's what I propose. We all walk up to the house, with Angie in the lead, then Marybeth and Sean because Rebecca already knows you. Then you and I, Josh, hanging back a bit. What do you think?"

"Sounds good so far," Josh concurred. "Then what?"

"I have no idea. That's all I got."

"Great." Josh tried to sound optimistic. "Sean, this is your ball game. Any suggestions?"

149

"I say we let Angie open the conversation and go from there. Angie, it is critically important that you do NOT freak out. We don't need to make everyone any more on edge than they already are. Least of all James. Do you hear me?"

"I got it. I can do this. Tell me what to say or not say."

"I think that if you just reassure them that we are not scammers, that we are friends of yours and that they should listen to us, I can take it from there."

"Okay. I can do that."

Just then, the GPS announced, "*You have arrived.*" They all took a collective deep breath.

Rebecca spotted them walking up the drive from the kitchen window.

"Mike," she called from the door, "You need to get in here."

Mike made it to the kitchen just as Angie climbed the back stairs. Rebecca immediately opened the door.

"Angie, what in heavens name are you doing here?" She gave her big hug but then backed off, eyeing the entourage accompanying her.

"Hi Aunt Becky. We need to come in."

"How do you know these people? They're not trying to scam you, too, are they?"

"No Aunt Becky. Honest. These people are friends of mine. MB owns the store where I work. They're good people. Please Aunt Becky. Can we come in?"

Rebecca turned to Mike who was standing right behind her.

"I'm assuming one of these guys is Sean." He looked at Becky for the answer.

"Yes."

He turned to the group. "Okay. But you have to know I have a short fuse for this." It was a clear warning. Mike was in charge and there would be no bull shit.

Rebecca stood aside, waving them in.

They cautiously entered a large country-style kitchen with a small table in the center. Rebecca didn't offer them a seat.

"Why didn't you come with them yesterday?" Rebecca asked Angie.

"Because we just figured out that James was Jimmy. I had no idea that Uncle Mike wasn't his dad."

Rebecca hesitated a moment. "That was a long time ago. And Uncle Mike *is* his dad."

"I know that," Angie agreed sympathetically, shooting a glance and a nod to Mike. "Anyway, there's no scam."

"Hi. I'm Sean." He extended his hand to Mike who accepted it. Sean gestured behind him with introductions. "This is my daughter, Marybeth, her boyfriend Josh, and my friend Ray." Nods were exchanged in recognition.

"You upset my wife yesterday, Sean, and I have to be honest, I'm not happy about that." Mike was staring him down.

"Yes. I'm sure I did." He turned to Rebecca. "I'm truly sorry for yesterday. I know it didn't go well. I really didn't know how else to handle this."

"Handle what?" Mike was not letting down his guard one bit.

Angie jumped in. "It's about Jimmy. Is he home?"

"No." It was a cautious reply from Rebecca with no other explanation.

Angie shot a pleading look at Rebecca.

Rebecca moved forward with polite formality.

"Please have a seat. Angie, go grab a couple of chairs from the dining room." Josh followed Angie to retrieve the chairs.

"Would anyone like some coffee?"

"We'd love some," the group said almost in unison.

"I'll get it Aunt Becky." Angie knew her way around Aunt Becky's kitchen as well as her own.

There was painful small talk while everyone got settled.

Sean took the lead. "I'm sorry this all sounds so mysterious." He paused, waiting for any push-back. Getting none, he pressed on. "I'm afraid it's going to get worse before it gets better."

Sean proceeded to give Rebecca and Mike a somewhat sanitized version of recent and past events, leaving out what he could. When he was done, there was a long silence at the table.

"So, you are asking me to believe that you have heard the voice of my long-dead husband telling you to help my son and that your daughter saw him at a yard sale where he gave her his helmet and letters."

"In a nutshell, yes," Sean nodded.

Marybeth stepped in for the first time. "I know it's a lot to take in. It is for us too."

"And where are these letters? So far, we've only seen the helmet and frankly that can be faked." Mike still sounded suspicious.

"Oh my God." Marybeth hit the table with her hand in surprised remembrance, startling everyone. "The letters. I completely forgot about them." She looked around for her purse. "I've got them right here." Reaching into the Bottomless Pit, she pulled out the fancy pouch. She removed the letters and journal and placed them on the table.

Rebecca sat frozen, staring at her own letters and the journal she had given Bobby before he left. There was a long moment when no one moved. Then Rebecca picked up the letters and froze. She immediately heard Bobby's voice.

Hello my love. You're beautiful as ever but we don't have time to reminisce. Sean is here to help James. Please let him. Do whatever he asks. Trust him.

Rebecca drops the letters and gasps. "Oh my God, I heard him."

Mike went into protection mode and demanded, "What kind of a joke is this?"

Angie reassures him, "Really, Uncle Mike. It's no joke and James is in real trouble. Please listen."

Sean turned his attention to Rebecca and gently asked, "What did he say?"

"He said I should trust you and that James needs your help."

"And what do you think about that?"

"I know James is in trouble. I've known it since the day he got home. I don't know what to do to help him."

"I do." It was a simple statement, but it broke the tension. Rebecca started to cry.

"Do you? Do you really? How can you know?" Rebecca sobbed.

"I know because I've been there. I've been angry at the world and I've been tired of living. I've been to war and I've come home and tried to put the pieces back together."

"He won't talk to you. He won't talk to anyone."

"Maybe. But I won't know till I try. And I have to try."

"We don't know where he is," she sobbed.

"Do you know when he'll be back?" Sean prodded.

It was Mike now. "He saw the helmet yesterday and Becks told him about your conversation. He got really angry and stormed out. We haven't seen him since."

"You haven't seen him since yesterday?" Angie was almost shrieking.

"Look," Mike defended himself. "The truth is, it's not uncommon, at least these days, for him go out and get drunk, then sleep it off in his Jeep somewhere. We're just figuring he'll be back when he's ready."

Sean's calm voice turned the conversation around. "Rebecca?"

She nodded.

"Can you pick the letters back up and see if Bobby knows where James is?"

"She most certainly cannot," Mike countered.

Rebecca pulled herself together. "It's okay Mike. It wasn't a bad thing. It just startled me is all."

"Are you sure?"

"Yes." She reached for the stack tied neatly with the twine. Immediately she felt Bobby's presence. Then she heard his voice.

I'm sorry I startled you.

"It's okay Bobby," Rebecca was fighting the sobs. The others looked on, only hearing one side of the conversation.

I'm sorry for a lot of things.

"What could you possibly have to be sorry for?"

Mostly I'm sorry I left you and James all alone. It couldn't have been easy for you.

"Don't be ridiculous, Bobby. You didn't leave us. You DIED."

Somehow it feels like it's my fault. Like I should have been more careful, should have made other choices, should have said I love you more often.

Rebecca was back to sobbing now. "Sean, you said you were with Bobby the day he died."

"Yes."

"Will you please tell him that it's not his fault he's dead."

"What? Bobby are you kidding?" Sean said to the air. "Unless you can see a mortar coming with enough time to dodge to the side, then no. It's not your fault you dumb-ass. You got on me for hanging on to stupid shit for years. Well, back atcha. Let it go, man."

Now that he puts it like that, it does sound a little stupid, but it's the way I've been feeling ever since I got here.

"It's not your fault Bobby and I never felt that way, not once."

I see you did as I asked. Mike has been a fine dad. Even now, in the dark times for James. And he's good to you, too.

"Yes, he is. We're both doing our best. But we don't know what else to do."

Sean does. He can help.

"But we don't know where he is."

Angie knows.

"How does she know?"

She just does. I can't explain, but they need to get going. James is sinking fast. He has a gun.

"Oh, Sweet Mother of God, pray for us."

She is. I have to go now.

"No Bobby," she cried. "Don't go," but there was only the silence of the kitchen while the group looked on, waiting for any new information. Rebecca cried, feeling the loss all over again.

Sean eased in as best he could. "I'm sorry Rebecca, but did Bobby say anything that can help us?"

"He said Angie knows where he is."

"Whaaaattt? How am I supposed to know?"

"You have to know, Angie," Rebecca pleaded.

"I haven't even seen him for years."

"Think, Angie," Marybeth said quietly, "Is there anything that comes to mind?"

"Nooooooo."

"It's a place that you both know, maybe from childhood," Marybeth prodded.

"And likely isolated," Sean added.

"Oh my God, I don't know! That was so long ago! Damn it Jimmy!" she yelled into the air.

Marybeth put a hand on her arm. "Think Angie. Where was your secret fort or clubhouse or something?

"There was a path in the woods," Angie recalled, "that lead to a huge tree. Jimmy showed me how to climb it. It was out behind that grocery store. Aunt Becky, you remember."

"I know where you mean. They cleared that out years ago and built a small park called Jefferson Commons, but there's still a few trees in the back. No one uses it much anymore. It's been all but abandon by the city. The cops don't even bother chasing the drunks out anymore."

"Yeah. That's got to be it." Angie was energized. "Okay. Let's go." She started to get up.

"Just a minute," Sean countered. "You're not going anywhere. You need to stay here with your Aunt and Uncle."

"Hell I do."

Before the argument could go any further there was a knock at the door that jolted them all out of current conversation. Mike opened the door to find Angie's mom, Nina.

"Mom? What are you doing here?"

"After that phone call, you didn't think I was going to sit at home waiting for something to happen, did you? I figured it had something to do with Aunt Becky and Jim so here I am. And clearly something is up."

Sean stood up. "I'm sorry but we don't have time to explain. We're all," he turned to Angie, "going to look for James. Please stay here with Rebecca and Mike. They can fill you in." As if on cue, the others stood to follow Sean out.

"Sean."

He turned to Rebecca.

"He has a gun."

He nodded understanding and they were gone.

"Who has a gun?" Nina cried. "James? Sweet Mother of God pray for us."

"She is," Rebecca replied.

Chapter 24

They got to the park quickly and pulled into a long-neglected parking lot that was now more pothole and dirt than asphalt. As predicted the area exemplified neglect and disrepair. Along one side was a chain link fence backing the shopping center adjacent to it. It acted like a net for plastic shopping bags and other loose debris carried on the wind. Picnic tables were stained with spilled beverages and animal droppings. A swing set stood in the center, minus two swings. The remaining one rusted and stiff in the wind.

Sean and Ray, seated in the front, did a quick visual sweep of the surrounds. The area was deserted except for a homeless guy asleep on a bench, and another sitting quietly on the edge of the playground with his shopping cart, watching them. He was about sixty, wearing an old army jacket and a baseball cap that said Vietnam Vet on it. Sean looked at Ray. Ray looked at Sean. The slightest of nods passed between them.

"Shit! I don't see him anywhere." Angie's head now stuck between the two of them from the back seat. Panic was taking over again.

"Wait. There's a car in the back corner. See it. Over there. Is that a jeep?" Ray was pointing to the furthest end of the park, where the neglected landscaping met the tree line.

"Looks like it." Sean confirmed. "Okay, we need to drive over there slowly."

"Do you think he's in there?" Angie was wringing her hands.

"I don't know," Sean said thoughtfully, "but at this point we need to consider that he's armed and, if not dangerous, then at least jumpy."

Ray leaned over and opened the love box. Inside was a white cloth with something wrapped inside. It was a hand gun.

Marybeth and Angie both reacted immediately.

"What is that?" They were talking over each other.

Ray turned around to the back seat with an expression that meant business. "Look. We are going into an unpredictable situation. I don't want an emotionally unstable vet to be the only person with a gun." Ray's voice was calm but final.

"You are not going to shoot him, are you?" Angie's eyes were wide with fear.

"As long as he isn't pointing a gun at himself or anyone else, no. I'm not."

"You mean if he's pointing it at himself, you're going to shoot?" Marybeth wasn't following that logic.

"Well, if I shoot him, he's more likely to survive, than if he shoots himself."

There was a pause while the seriousness of the situation set in. He went on with the same tone of absolute authority. "*And* I don't want to go into this with someone who is panicking and likely to go off in a crazy counterproductive rant – ANGIE." He looked her straight in the eyes and spoke slowly. "So, if you can't pull it together, stay in the car. We don't need you fueling something that's already on fire."

Angie was stunned. Sean tried to take some of the sting out.

"He's right Angie. You've got to calm down. Can you do that?"

Angie took a long deep breath. "Okay. I get it." Another deep breath. "I'm good."

"And you have to let me handle it. Do you understand?" Sean insisted she reply.

"Yes, Sean. Yes. I get it. Stay calm. Shut up. I can do this." The last statement seemed as much to herself as to Sean.

Sean turned to Ray. "Okay?"

Ray gave the same slight nod as before.

Marybeth caught it this time. It was a soldier's nod.

Ray drove slowly to the end of the lot. As they got closer, it became clear that James was not in the jeep.

"Angie, do you remember where the path was?" Sean asked calmly.

"Oh God. Let me think. It looks all different."

"What *do* you remember?" Marybeth prodded gently.

"I remember a little patch of daisies, and an old rotting log, and a huge elm tree that marked the path."

"Like that?" Ray pointed to a tall tree towering over the others at the edge of the park.

"Yeah," Angie leaned forward and studied it. "Yeah. Like that. And look. You can see the trail just to the left. People must still use it."

Ray pulled up beside the jeep and parked.

"What else do you remember?" Sean prompted this time. "Is this climbing tree in a clearing? At the edge of a brook? Any detail is helpful."

161

"Yes. A clearing. And at the far side is an old railroad track. It's not used any more. Not even then."

Sean took control. "Here's how this is going to go. I'll head down the trail first. Angie, you behind me. When I tell you to, start calling James' name and say who you are. 'Hey James. It's me, Angie.' You got it?"

"Yes."

"Ray, you're following Angie." Ray gave a nod.

"Marybeth and Josh, I'd like you to both stay here but know that's not likely."

"Nope." They both replied at once.

"So, please hang back a bit. We don't want to overwhelm him. Marybeth, you're the one who saw Bobby, so I might ask you to step in."

"Got it."

"Josh, if you see anything that we don't that indicates it's getting dangerous, step in."

"And Josh," Sean looked him straight in the eye, "you're looking out for my daughter."

"Every minute, Sean." Josh reassured him.

"Alright. Let's go talk to James."

As they got out of the Tahoe, Ray tucked the gun in the back waistband of his jeans.

Meanwhile, unnoticed, the way most homeless people are, the Vet had abandoned his cart and moved to the edge of the park. He watched them as they entered the woods, then silently followed them in, out of sight. He was carrying a baseball bat.

They walked in silence down the trail. When Sean saw the clearing ahead, he motioned for Angie to call out.

"Hey, Jimmy. It's me, Angie. Jimmy? Are you here?'

There was no response as they entered the clearing. Sean motioned Angie again.

"Jimmy? Are you here? It's me, Angie."

Sean spotted him first, sitting on the old tracks at the far side of the clearing, about thirty feet away. His arms were resting on his knees as he stared at the ground. Sean stopped the group.

He whispered back to Josh. "What's he look like?"

Josh studied James for a moment. "He's very dark and compressed."

Angie inhaled sharply but refrained from saying anything.

Josh heard it and reassured them all. "No. That's good. It shows that he's unhappy, struggling, fearful."

They all looked at him strangely.

"If he were committed to this, he would be golden glowy happy, relieved to have made the decision. It means there's talking room."

They all let out their breath. Sean motioned them to move forward slowly.

"What are you doing here, Angie?" Jimmy called out before they got half way across. He ran his fingers through his hair but didn't look up.

"I was worried about you," Angie called back.

"Well, don't. I'm fine."

"Ah, well, I'm thinking not."

Sean motioned for group to hang back as he moved forward.

"Hi James. My name's Sean. I served with your dad in Vietnam."

"Big fucking deal."

"It was for me. He was a good man. He loved you."

"Again, big fucking deal."

Sean stopped at about fifteen feet away when he spotted the gun at James' feet.

"I found his helmet recently in some of my things. I thought you might want it."

"Well, I don't. What did he ever do for me? Nothing. He died a hero. Big fucking deal. I didn't get so lucky."

"The way I see it, you got luckier."

"How do you figure that?"

"You get to see your kids grow up."

James shifted a little at this but still didn't look up. "Well, maybe my kids aren't so lucky."

"Kids always want their dad. You know that. It's been true for you. Right?"

James got angry at this and looked up at Sean. "Look. If you're trying to make me feel bad, you're doing a great job."

"Maybe I *am* trying to make you feel bad, but for someone besides yourself."

"Shut up, man. You don't know shit about me."

"Maybe not. But I know about me. And I've sat where you sit, more than once."

Marybeth sucked a breath in. Josh reached out and took her hand. James immediately looked over at the movement, hesitated, then disregarded it.

"Oh, is this the *I know what you're going through* speech?"

"Nope. Just telling you a story."

When James didn't protest, Sean went on.

"I thought I was no good to anybody and that I was only making life harder for my family." He paused.

"Well, maybe that was true," James spat out.

"Oh, it was definitely true. I got an ex-wife that will testify to it."

James said nothing, staring back at the ground, and the gun.

"Do you want your kids to grow up like you did? Without a dad? Oh, I'm sure Mike is a good man but he's not your dad. Is that what you want for your kids? A stand-in dad?"

James got mad again. "Of course not! But I'm no good to them. I'm so fucked up I can't even think straight! What good is that?"

"You won't always be fucked up, James."

"Oh, yeah. I think I will. Nobody gets better from PTSD."

"I don't know why you think that, but it's completely untrue. I'm living proof."

"You're not LIKE ME!"

"Nope. I'm not. I spent the first four years back from Vietnam swallowing pills and washing them down with whatever whiskey was on sale that week."

Marybeth sucked in another breath. James looked up.

"Who's that?"

"That's my daughter."

James didn't respond.

"Say, James. If we're going to keep talking, do you suppose you can unload the gun. I'm not asking you to give it up. Just unload it, you know, for the safety of everyone else."

Everyone held their breath. Ray, in particular, watched very closely.

At first James just sat there. Then, slowly, he reached down and removed the clip from his gun and placed both pieces back on the ground at his feet.

"Thanks James. You know, you're right. I don't know your story. I only know mine and the story of a few others that I've talked to over the years. I can tell you that every one of us is glad we're still alive."

"Yeah, but would their families say that?"

"Again, I can only tell you my story. But you can ask my daughter if you like."

James said nothing. Sean motioned Marybeth to come forward.

"Hi James. I'm Marybeth. Sean's daughter. I was eight when my parents divorced and my dad finally got some help. I'm not going lie, there was a lot of craziness, but not always. We had good times too. No matter what, I never stopped loving my dad. I was angry at him for a long time and he put up with a lot of attitude from me, I'm sure." She glanced over at her dad who nodded her to keep going. "I never ever wished he were gone."

"So, great. One success story. Congratulations on your happy family."

Marybeth fought back frustration. "What I'm saying, James, is that your kids don't look at it the same way you do. They have kid's eyes and they think whatever is wrong is their fault." Sean took his eyes off James for a moment and looked over at Marybeth. She met his eyes with the quickest of glances and continued. "They love you. They want you to get better, not dead."

Sean waved her to hold up a minute.

Everyone was silent.

James held his head in his hands, and looking down said, "I can't help but think they'll be better off if I'm gone."

Angie, who had been true to her word until now, stepped toward him. James head snapped up when he heard the movement. Sean tried to stop her, but she dismissed him with a wave.

"No, Sean. *This* I got." She turned to James. "So, you think we'll all be better off without you?"

"Angie, you don't know anything about this." James tried to blow her off.

"I don't know about combat or about the Army. You're right. But I know about suicide." There was a palpable shock as the word hit the air. "There. I've said it out loud. That's what we're all doing here, isn't it? Well, I know a lot about *that*. More than I ever wanted to know. Do you want to know why?"

"What are you saying Angie. I don't understand."

"Jackie. Remember her? My sister? Your cousin?"

"Of course I remember Jackie. She died in a car accident."

Angie went on slowly and deliberately. "Jackie drove her car into a bridge abutment at sixty miles an hour."

There was a long silence while James physically twisted himself up with this information.

"Shit, Angie. I didn't know. I'm sorry."

"So, I know, Jimmy. And I'm telling you, life is not better without my sister." She paused to catch her own breath and fight back her tears. "It's been six years and there isn't a day that goes by that I don't think of her. For years I replayed every conversation I had with her, wondering what I missed, what I could have done, or, worse, what I did that made things worse. I was angry at her when she died. I'll never forgive myself for that."

"Angie, you gotta know, it's not your fault."

"Mostly I know that. But not all the way. I can't help but wonder the 'what ifs'. They attack me in the middle of the night. And it's not just me. My kids miss her. They think it was an accident so it's probably easier for them. Your kids won't think you accidentally blew your brains out. And none of us will be glad you're gone. We'll miss you. We'll miss you on your birthday, and on your kids' birthdays, and at Christmas and Thanksgiving and the Fourth of July picnic, and at weddings and christenings."

"Okay, STOP. STOP. STOP!" James and Angie were both in tears. "I just don't know what else to do!"

Sean motioned Angie to be quiet and picked up the conversation from here. "I do, James. I know what to do."

James remained silent.

"Why don't we go back to your mother's where we can talk more."

"She doesn't want me back."

"Of course she does," Sean countered. "Where do you think we came from. She's worried sick."

"Whaddaya say, Jimmy?" Angie pleaded.

James still didn't move.

"Look, James. You can kill yourself anytime you want. So how about just not today?"

"DAD!" Marybeth gasped at the comment.

"What? I'm just pointing out the facts. If James wants to kill himself tomorrow, nothing's stopping him." He turned to James. "And since you've got nothing but time, you might as well hear what we have to say. If you don't like it, you're free to do whatever you want tomorrow."

"You don't have to give him any ideas, Sean." Angie's voice was escalating.

"It's okay, Angie. Sean isn't saying anything I haven't thought about a hundred times."

"So, what do you say? Are you in?" Sean asked him.

"Okay, but it better be one hell of a conversation."

"You have no idea." Sean shook his head side to side.

James started to get up, then reached for his gun.

"You can leave that there." Sean stopped him. "My friend Ray will pick it up. He'll bring it back to the house. I promise."

James didn't argue. He got up and walked down from the tracks. As soon as he was on level ground, Angie launched herself at him, locking him into a bear hug that would put a grizzly to shame. James hugged her back.

The homeless man, who had taken up a silent surveillance from behind some trees, slid quietly back into the woods. Trails of tears could be seen through the dirt on his face if anyone had been there to look.

When they got to the parking lot, Sean laid out the evolving plan. "Ray and Josh can drive your car back, James. You can ride with us in the Tahoe."

James reached into his pocket and handed his keys to Ray. Ray, in turn, handed the Tahoe keys to Sean.

Sean turned to Angie. "Call your aunt please. Tell her we're all safe and coming in hungry."

Angie pulled out her phone. "Between her and my mom, I'm sure they're already cooking."

Chapter 25

Back in Rebecca's kitchen, Nina sat with her jaw hanging open while her sister recounted recent events, including hearing Bobby's voice.

"Oh, Becky. Surely you just imagined it."

"No. Bobby's voice went straight into my heart when I picked up those letters. I'll recognize it till the day I die." She glanced at Mike. "No offense."

"None taken." He reached across the table and took her hand.

They sat there for a moment, looking at the items on the table. No one wanted to touch them.

"You should have told me all this before," Nina admonished her.

"What would you have done?"

"I'd have come over and cried with you." Nina stated the obvious.

"Well, here's your chance."

"What? You mean we just sit around waiting?"

"That's what we've been doing since yesterday."

"Oh, no, no, no. Those people are bringing Jimmy back right now. I know it. And he's going to be hungry. So are they. So, let's get cooking."

"What?" Rebecca started to protest.

"You heard me. What do you have around here?" Nina was opening cabinets and rooting through the refrigerator before Rebecca could get out of the chair.

"You're right. Of course. Let's get to it."

Mike got up and headed for the living room. "And that's my cue to get out of the kitchen."

They were just taking the Chicken Parmesan and roasted vegetables out of the oven when the phone rang. Rebecca raced to it.

"Hello?"

Rebecca was listened silently for a minute while Nina and Mike waited impatiently for news.

"Oh, thank God. So, everyone's okay?" She paused to listen. "And you're headed back here?" She paused again. "Well, you're in luck. Your mom and I just finished cooking. We'll put the spaghetti on when you get here."

Mike and Nina let out their breath. "Are they okay? What happened?" They both jumped on Rebecca immediately.

"Whoa." She held her hands up waving them off. "Yes. Everyone is fine. I don't know anything else except he was at the park and they are heading here. In five minutes, you can ask them everything yourselves."

Jimmy came through the door first and Rebecca grabbed him in her arms and wouldn't let go.

After giving her a light hug, Jimmy squirmed to get loose.

"Mom. MOM. Come on. Let go."

She loosened her grip. "I'm sorry. I'm sorry. I've just been so frightened, Jimmy. Are you okay, honey?" She touched his face tenderly.

"No, Mom. I'm not okay." He shook her off.

"I'm sorry, James." She was close to tears.

Mike stepped in. "Stop bullying your mother, Jimmy. What's wrong with you."

"It's okay, Mike. Just leave it." Rebecca defended him.

"No, it's not okay," Mike insisted.

"Dad's right, Mom. I'm sorry. See? This is what I mean," he turned to Sean. "I make a mess of everything."

Sean looked around at everyone as he spoke. "Emotions are high for all of us right now. I say we all just take a few minutes to calm down and have something to eat because it smells amazing in here."

"I second that," Nina chirped from the stove. "And in the meantime, get out of my kitchen."

"Who's kitchen?" Rebecca demanded, feigning indignation. It was enough to break the tension. The men instinctively moved to the living room while the women remained to attend to the food. Not wanting to interrupt the cooks, Marybeth busied herself with setting the table in the dining room. The letters were forgotten for the moment, buried under coats and purses on the kitchen table.

The meal was delicious, and everyone was on their best behavior. Becky and Nina shared family stories from happier times, embarrassing Angie and Jim, alternately. The guys swapped a few Army stories, but everyone was cautious to stay away from any touchy subjects. As the dishes were cleared, the group moved to the living room for coffee. Marybeth spotted the helmet and letters on her way out of the kitchen and grabbed them all, stuffing the letters and journal back in the pouch.

Chatter in the living room quieted when she placed the items on the coffee table. James gingerly reached for the helmet.

"Wait James." Sean touched his arm from behind, causing James to jump. "Sorry, but there's a few things you need to know before you touch anything."

James looked at him suspiciously. "What do you mean?"

Mike responded. "Jimmy, there's been a lot of crazy things happening since yesterday. I think it's better if we talk first. Sean, maybe you should start off."

"Like I said before," Sean began, "I knew your father." Sean paused, glancing up at Mike. "No disrespect."

"None taken." Mike assured him.

"We spent some time together in Danang when his unit was in for supplies," Sean continued. "I was stationed there, in charge of shipping home dead soldiers." Sean collected his thoughts for a moment deciding how to go forward. "A lot of strange things happen in war." Sean hesitated again. James jumped in.

"You don't think I know that." He was getting frustrated already.

"I know you do, James, but I have to tell the story the way I have to tell it." Sean waited while James forced himself into an uncomfortable patience. "Your dad and I both had unusual experiences over there. Mine was that I could hear the voices of dead soldiers."

James began to protest. "What?" He looked up at Mike for either confirmation or contradiction.

"I know it sounds crazy, Jim, but hear him out," Mike encouraged.

James turned to Sean. "Alright Sean, but you gotta know my patience is really short."

"I'll do my best to get to the point. I know this sounds crazy but please keep an open mind."

James gave him the soldier's nod.

"I'll tell you the whole story another time, but for now I'll just say that Bobby, your father, reached out to me when he saw that you were in trouble."

"What? This is some bullshit. Are you trying to trick me into something?" James demanded. Ray adjusted his posture ever so slightly in response to James' agitation. James noticed the move, assessed Ray quickly and settled himself down again.

"No. James. I assure you. There's no trick. This is my truth. How else would I even be here?"

James had already considered the unlikely coincidence of a friend of his dead father showing up at this particular moment.

When James was quiet, Sean went on, "My daughter brought me a helmet and these letters..."

"How'd she get them?" James interrupted.

"That's her story to tell and she will. In any case, when I picked up the helmet, I heard Bobby's voice telling me you were in trouble. With help from some friends at the VA, we tracked your mother down. When we gave her the letters, your dad talked to her."

James tensed up again. Ray matched him, move for move, ready to intervene if needed. He looked to Mike.

"It's true, Jim. I can't say I understand any of it. But your mom says it happened. That's how we knew where you were. Well, Angie knew."

"This is crazy shit! You guys know that, right?" James looked around for agreement for someone, anyone.

"I told you, you would need an open mind, James. Just stay with me."

James remained silent but still jumpy.

Sean went on, "I'm telling you this because if you pick up the helmet, you might hear something or you might not. I don't know. But if you do, you need to know that you're not losing your mind."

"That ship fuckin' sailed months ago."

"No, it didn't James. You're not crazy. You're just trying to understand things that are confusing."

"You don't know how bad it is, Sean." James shook his head, wondering what the hell was happening to him.

"No, but I can guess."

James looked at the helmet. "Are you saying that if I pick up that helmet, I can talk to my dad?"

"I can only say maybe."

Most of the tension had drained out of James' body and his emotions had shifted to a familiar despair as he reached out for the helmet.

James, my baby boy. Look at you. A full-grown man. I'm so proud of you, son.

Tears welled up in James' eyes. He looked around at the others.

"We can't hear him James. Just you," Sean replied to the unasked question.

I'm sorry I couldn't be there to see you grow up, play catch, go fishing.

"So why are you showing up now? After forty years!" James was speaking out loud.

I can't say I understand any of it. But I never got over losing you and your mother. Not even over here. I think that's what reconnected us somehow, when you started feeling desperate and hopeless. I remember just before I died, I had the same feelings, desperate and hopeless that I would never get to see you again.

"Lately I started to envy you. Death seems easier right now." James was staring off into nowhere as he spoke.

It might seem like the easy way, James, but it's not the right way. First of all, your family needs you. Secondly, you have to deal with shit over here too. Death isn't a free pass. Look at me. I've been hanging on to this grief for forty years. It took your crisis to make me see how wonderful your life has been - and is. Mike has been an exceptional father and I can finally be happy for you and your mom.

"But I'm no good to anyone." James was in tears.

Maybe not right now. But this will pass, and you will be a great dad to your own kids.

"I can't see how."

Sean can help. You don't have to reinvent the wheel. You have to learn how to trust those who have already walked the path. You younger vets think the old guys don't understand but they do. Take the help.

"Alright. I'll give it a try."

I know you don't know me, James, but I know you. I saw you take your first breath. You were so small I was afraid to hold you, thinking I would break you or something. Your mother laughed at me. Anyway, the journal is for you. It will tell you a little about me and how much you meant to me. The letters are for your mother. I love you, son.

James put the helmet down. "Wow. That was crazy even for me."

Rebecca was the first to ask. "What did he say, Jim?"

"He said he never stopped loving us and missing us. He said that Mike was a great dad. And he said I should let Sean help me."

Sean heaved a sigh of relief. "And what do you say?"

"Well, it's hard to argue with that." He pointed to the helmet. "I don't even know where to start though."

"Do you have your VA benefits set up?"

"I haven't actually checked in yet."

"Then we'll go tomorrow and get things going."

Rebecca protested. "What's the rush. Can't he have a few days to take all this in?"

"Not really. James isn't going to feel any better until he gets some help."

"We can take him down next week." Mike offered.

Sean looked over at James for comment.

"No, Mom. Sean's right. I've been putting it off for months, maybe longer if I were honest. If I'm going to do this, it's gotta be now, especially after Angie told me about how Jackie really died."

Angie gasped. Nina gasped. They looked at each other.

James started to get nervous. "Oh, no. Did I say something wrong? Damn it!"

"Mom, I'm sorry I never told you."

"Angie, I didn't know that you knew."

"How do *you* know?" Angie asked her mom.

"Honey, I read the police report. They didn't come right out and say it, but all the implications were there."

"Mom, I never said anything because I didn't want to upset you."

Rebecca stood up, disrupting the conversation. "What are you both talking about? What about Jackie?" she demanded.

Nina answered the question. "The police believed that Jackie drove herself into that bridge. On purpose."

"What? That's ridiculous," argued Rebecca.

"I'm sorry, Becky, for not telling you. It's just that, well, I guess we'll never know for sure, so I like to think it was something else."

"Oh my God." Rebecca collapsed back onto her chair. Then she looked up at James with panic creeping over her face.

"Mom, I swear, I won't do it. Believe me. After today, I got the message. Please don't worry."

She put her head in her hands. "God, will this day ever end?"

"Yes. In fact, right now. This day ends now. We've all been through enough already." Mike took charge again.

"I agree," Sean chimed in. "We've all had a long day."

"Hold up. Wait just a minute." It was Jimmy. "My puzzle has a lot of pieces missing. I have a hundred questions."

"I promise we'll fill in the details another time. How about if Ray and I pick you up tomorrow at eleven. We'll have to go to Philadelphia to start with, but then you can probably hook up with the Vet Center here in Harrisburg." Sean looked over at Ray for confirmation.

"Yeah, that works for me. We can fill in some of those pieces on the way." Ray nodded agreement. They turned to James.

"I can live with that," James answered without thinking. The inadvertent play on words caused an awkward moment. "Anyway, thanks."

They all exchanged goodbyes and the Pomroy contingent headed home. All except for Angie who elected to stay the night at her mom's.

Chapter 26

The next day, Ray and Sean headed out early to Harrisburg. They had a couple of stops to make before picking up James. First stop, three coffees, donuts and a breakfast sandwich to go, from the Hot Topics Cafe. As an afterthought, they added a hoagie and bottle of soda to the order, then headed back to the Tahoe.

As hoped, the old vet was sitting alone in Jefferson Commons at one of the cement tables. The baseball bat had been returned to its place in the cart, not obvious, but within easy access. They approached him slowly and kept a respectful distance.

"Good morning, sir," Sean offered as a greeting.

"So you say." The man looked them both up and down, eyeing the coffee and bags of take-out.

"We thought you might want breakfast." Sean offered the bags as Ray pulled a coffee out of the cardboard tray and offered it to him. He and Sean took the other two.

"Cream and sugar. We were guessing." Ray was almost apologetic.

"It don't matter to me," the old guy said without meeting their eyes. He cautiously accepted the cup and bags.

"We were here yesterday..." Ray started.

"Yeah. I saw ya. Helping out that guy in the woods."

"You saw that?" Ray was surprised.

"Course I did." The answer was gruff and irritated. "Homeless people aren't stupid. I see three guys with a gun take two women into the woods and I get a little curious. See?"

"I do see, now that you put it that way." Ray was nodding his head. "Why didn't you say something?"

"I listened. Turned out it was none of my business." The man shrugged.

"My friend Sean and I couldn't help notice your hat yesterday. Did you serve in Vietnam?"

"I was with the 3rd Marines in '68 in Khe Sahn. You?"

"82nd Airborne, '69. I was all over the place."

"Medic, '69, Danang." Sean chimed in reluctantly.

The old vet huffed.

"I know. I'm sorry." Sean always felt he had to apologize for his relatively safe tour in-country.

"No need to apologize," the old man said. "It was the luck of the draw for all of us."

"It didn't stop me from getting blown up and sent home, if it's worth anything."

"Sorry to hear it. Did that guy's dad die in Nam?" The old man changed the subject.

"Yeah. I knew him over there. He was a hometown boy though. Bobby McMillan."

"Who?" the homeless man perked up at the name.

"Bobby McMillan. Did you know him?"

"He was a friend of mine in high school. We played basketball together. He wasn't that tall but he was wiry, twisting and turning around all the tall guys." The man moved his shoulders back and forth slightly, demonstrating the moves. Then he got quiet. "Our draft numbers were one number apart. We went in together and got assigned to the same unit. We stayed together for a while, but you know how chaotic it was over there. Eventually we got split up. Sorry to know he didn't make it back. He used to talk about his baby boy all the time. He served in the middle east?"

"Iraq and Afghanistan."

"That's a different kind of war than ours."

"Different and the same," Sean mused.

"Did you mean what you said to him yesterday, about knowing how to get the demons out of your head?"

"I know how I did it," Sean replied. "Are you interested?"

"Maybe. Sometimes I think I'm too old to wrestle that bear. You know, why bother?"

"Your family might think there's a reason," Ray pondered, looking off into the distance to avoid appearing confrontational.

The man was quiet.

Ray extended his hand. "My name's Ray. This is Sean. We'd like to help you out. If you're interested."

"Let's say I was. What would be the first thing?"

"Well, first you'd have to be registered at the VA in Philly. Are you listed with them?"

"If I was, it was a long time ago. I'd probably have to do it all again."

"We can take you down if you like."

"I can't leave my stuff," he quickly replied.

Ray thought about it for a minute. "What if we could get the Vet Center here in town to look after it for a few hours while we're gone? Would that work? And maybe you could get a little cleaned up there before we leave?"

"Ha," the man chuckled. "What are you saying? I stink?"

"Well, sir, I'm not going to lie. It's a long drive to Philadelphia."

The old man chuckled again and nodded. "Alright, but only if my stuff will be safe."

"We'll make sure of it," Sean reassured him.

"Why don't we pick you up there on Thursday?" Ray offered.

"Sure. That'd be fine."

"Great." Sean extended his hand for a handshake. "What's our name, soldier?"

"Dean."

"Okay, Dean. We'll see you then."

They were walking away when Dean called out, "Hey?"

They turned.

"Do you think that boy would like to hear about his dad?"

"I'm sure he would." Sean gave the nod.

Their next stop was the closest department store. They guessed at Dean's sizes and got him some clean clothes to wear to Philadelphia along with some travel size personal hygiene products and a towel. Then they headed to the Vet Center. As they expected, the social worker, Denise, was more than happy to help.

"Dean? Oh sure," she said. "He comes by here from time to time. I keep telling him he's got to get to Philadelphia before we can do much for him. Then I give him whatever food I have, and he shuffles off. You guys know him?"

"Not really," Ray acknowledged. "We spotted him yesterday in the park and went by this morning to talk. We're just couple of vets helping out one of our own."

"Are you sure he's a vet?"

They weren't offended by the question. The sad truth is that a lot of people falsely claim to be vets.

"Pretty sure. He identified his unit and location without any trouble."

"Glad to hear it. He always seemed like the real deal. I'm glad you guys are helping out." She flashed Ray a smile. "Guys like Dean get frustrated quickly and won't follow through. Mostly they just need someone to literally walk them through the process."

Ray gave her a flirty wink in return. "That's what we're hoping for. And it's good that he already knows you."

"He does. I've been wanting to get him some help for a couple of years. I'm looking forward to it." She paused, then, "So, I'll be seeing more of you then?" she looked directly at Ray, suppressing a smile.

"Yes, you will," Ray smiled back. "Maybe we can have lunch on one of those occasions?"

"It could happen," she nodded, not breaking eye contact.

"Hm-hm," Sean cleared his throat. "Thanks for your help, Denise, but we have other business today, so we'll be going."

"Oh, yeah," Ray agreed. "It was a pleasure to meet you." He tipped his cowboy hat with a nod.

"Likewise. And thank you for what you're doing for Dean."

"Our pleasure," Sean replied as he ushered Ray out the office door and down the hallway.

"Well, that was productive," Sean noted.

"It certainly was." Ray was still smiling as left the building.

Chapter 27

Angie stayed the night with her mom. They talked about all the things they hadn't talked about for the past six years. They cried and laughed and told stories from the past. In the morning they headed back over to Becky's to spend time with family. When they got there, Becky was cleaning up after breakfast, Jimmy was on the way to Philadelphia with Sean and Ray, and Mike was off to work.

They helped themselves to coffee, headed into the living room and settled in around the coffee table where the helmet and pouch still sat from the day before. The journal was moved to one of the end tables.

"Aunt Becky, did you look at the journal?"

"No. I haven't had the heart. James was reading it when I got up this morning."

"And you haven't opened the letters yet either?"

"No."

"Why not? I'd be all over them." Angie couldn't understand her aunt's hesitation.

"Considering what happened yesterday when I picked them up, I guess I'm a little nervous. I thought maybe we could look at them together."

"Sure thing." Angie reached out for the pouch.

"Angie!" her mother admonished, "let Aunt Becky handle her own business, please."

"Oh, right. Sorry Aunt Becky."

Becky reached out for the pouch and spilled the letters out onto the table. Spreading them out, she spotted a delicate silver chain. She fished it out and cupped the medallion gently in her hand, shielding it from view.

"What's that Becca?" Nina used an old pet name for her sister.

"I don't know. I've never seen it before." She held it up and let it dangle free.

Angie's stared at it in disbelief. "What? Can I see that?" She held out her hand and cradled the medallion the way Becky had. "Oh my God. This can't be true."

Next thing she knew, she had an unexpected voice in her head.

Hello Angie. This is Bobby. Don't be alarmed. I have a message from your sister, Jackie.

"What? How is this possible?"

"How is what possible, honey?" her mother asked.

"I have a voice in my head. He says he's Bobby."

Becky could hear Angie's anxiety rising. "It's okay, dear. It's just a little off-putting at first."

I saw Jackie just before she crossed over from here.

"What do you mean from there? That's not the end?"

No. It's just a place along the journey. It's not a bad place, it's just not the end. After we leave our bodies, we are asked to let go of all remaining attachments to our physical life. Some souls take longer than others, but time is different here. I've been holding onto my love and sadness over losing my family. It took recent events for me to understand that they are fine and in good hands.

"So why the necklace?"

Jackie let go of things the day she was able to get that message to you last year. Before she left, she asked me that if I should ever get the chance to communicate with you that I should give you this and remind you that she loves you. I have to go now. Be a beacon of light for those who are going through what you have already experienced. Tell your Aunt Becky I love her. It's all in the letters.

"Wait! I have a hundred questions." She heard a faint swoosh of air and then silence. "Bobby? Bobby? Wait!" There was only silence.

She looked up to see her mom and Aunt Becky looking at her.

"Are you alright?" Her mother was clearly concerned.

"Yes. I'm fine. Really. It was definitely weird though."

"What happened?"

"I was talking to Bobby." She shook her head at the impossibility of the statement.

Rebecca looked around as if for some sign.

"He's gone now. He asked me to tell you that he loves you. And that he's able to move on now because he knows you're all safe. He said it's all in the letters." Angie looked down at the table, "but I don't understand. These are letters from you to him." She was looking at Becky, who gave her a sad smile and nodded understanding.

Without a word, she got up and walked over to a window seat that served as a storage bench. After moving things around, she returned to the couch with an old shoe box. Inside was a bundle of letters tied with ribbon.

"He's talking about these. His letters to me."

"Wow." A silence settled over the room. There was the whole story laid out. Two sets of letters and a journal telling the story of two young lovers.

"Wow," Angie said again.

Becky stacked them together and put them aside. "I'll look at them later."

"Of course, Becky. Let me know if you need anything." Nina turned her attention to Angie. "What about the necklace?" Mom prodded her.

"It was Jackie's. I have one just like it, almost." She reached into her pocketbook and retrieved her key ring. "I have mine on my keys. See? It's our birth stones." Angie showed them a similar medallion but with a black onyx stone."

Your birth stone is a ruby," Mom corrected. "And Jackie's is a sapphire."

"I know. These are our zodiac birth stones. Peridot for me and onyx for Jackie. We used to read our horoscopes all the time. We exchanged these charms when she graduated high school, so we would always be connected."

"Bobby said that after she messaged me last year, she was able to move on."

"What? What message?" Mom was almost demanding an answer.

"Well, in light of recent events, I guess I'll tell you a little of the back story." Angie proceeded to tell the tale of last year's yard sale and the cell phone message she received from Jackie. When she was finished, no one doubted her.

Chapter 28

Josh awoke to the smell of coffee and bacon. For a moment he wasn't sure where he was. He rolled over to find himself alone in bed. Was Marybeth cooking breakfast? That would be a first. But it was the only logical answer. He got up quietly and peeked around the corner into the kitchen.

There was Marybeth, at the stove in front of a large frying pan.

"Hey?" He ventured into the room.

"Hey, yourself." She didn't take her eyes off the bacon.

"What are you doing?"

"What does it look like I'm doing?"

"I'm not sure. I've never seen you actually do this."

"You've seen me cook before." She was getting a little defensive.

"Yes. Just not before noon."

"Well, I've been thinking a lot about our talk the other day and I feel bad about it."

"So, is this guilt cooking?"

191

"Not exactly, but I do admit that I take you for granted sometimes and I'm sorry for that."

"Okay."

"And I want to talk about things this morning, but you always insist we eat first. So, let's eat."

"Okay then. Can I help?"

"Nope. I'm just going to scramble some eggs. Toast is buttered and on the table.

He turned to look and, sure enough, there is was. He was impressed. "Wow. This is great. Thank you." He kissed her cheek as he headed for the coffee pot. "You know you're setting a precedent here?"

"For cooking breakfast or talking?"

"Both."

"Maybe. Don't raise your expectations too high."

"Got it."

They spent the next hour deconstructing the events of yesterday and wondering what was next for James. The whole thing seemed unreal. When breakfast was done, they took their coffee to the living room.

"I wonder what it would be like to talk to my mother again," Josh mused.

"Stick with me. I'll probably bump into her again."

"Well, now that you bring it up...," Josh paused.

Marybeth felt her stomach begin to knot up. She willed herself to stay calm. "Yeah, us."

"Yeah."

"Look, can you start please?"

"Okay, here's the thing, MB. I'm looking for a long-term committed relationship."

"Isn't that what we have?"

"This doesn't feel very committed. It feels like you're still in the wait and see place. If this isn't the right relationship for you, you need to say so."

"I'm trying not to get my hopes up."

"And I'm trying to stay hopeful."

Marybeth could feel her anxiety rising. Her throat tightened, and her brain started slowing down. She took a deep breath. "I can't help but ask myself how much longer this is going to last. I keep waiting for some warning sign or confirmation or something. I can't seem to help it."

"So far, have there been any warning signs?"

"No."

"Maybe you can give yourself a more positive way to look at it."

"Like what?"

"Maybe you could start asking yourself what next great things will happen instead of wondering when disaster will strike."

"Okay. I can do that." She took another deep inhale.

"I'd like to look one year ahead and talk about what we expect."

"I haven't even looked one week ahead."

"Then I'm asking you to do that now."

"Okay. Again, can you start please. You seem to have already thought about it."

"I'd like a situation that doesn't require a four-hour drive to see each other."

Marybeth was getting frustrated fast. "I don't know what to say to that. This is why I hate talking about it. What do you want me to say?"

"I want to have a reasonable conversation about where this is going and what options we have over the next year or so. I'm just looking to entertain different ideas, you know, create our own measuring stick?"

"Look, Josh. Most of the time I try hard to not think about it. I over-thought my marriage. Planning, strategizing and calculating down to the minute. Look where it got me. This time I'm just trying to enjoy the moment."

"I understand, but I'm looking for something more. If not with you, then....," Josh shrugged his shoulders.

"Then what! Is this an ultimatum?" This was getting out of control quickly.

Josh tried to calm it back down. "We need to know where each of us stand on this. This isn't a marriage proposal, MB! It's just a conversation." Josh's voice was rising now too.

They sat there, neither one knowing what to say next. It was Josh who made the next move.

"I was thinking about getting an apartment here in town."

Again silence.

"Really MB? Maybe I had this all wrong. Sorry. My bad." Josh was done.

"No. no. You're not wrong."

"MB, it can't be this hard all the time to talk about important things."

"I know. I'm just not good at it. You don't understand what ten years of arguing does to a person's communication skills."

"At some point you have to stop blaming your marriage."

"Maybe, but now's not the time."

"MB?"

"Alright. Let's say you get an apartment here. What would that mean?"

"It would mean that we would spend more time together and see how that goes. I miss being with you when we're not together."

The honest comment plucked at her heartstrings. "I miss you too," she admitted.

"I'm not trying to rush things, but it is the nature of relationships to move forward. It's the nature of everything to move forward. The topic on the table is not whether we move forward or not, it's whether we move forward together or not. Nothing stays the same, ever."

She was silent for a long time, or at least if felt like a long time to Josh.

"Would you give up your house in Connecticut?"

"Not at first. I'll still need to go back and forth for a while in any event. But I'll spend most of my time here."

"And when would you make this move?"

"Not till after the holidays."

"Okay. I can live with that," she relaxed a little.

"I don't want you to live with it." Josh was doing his best to keep the irritation from his voice. "I want you to embrace it. Be excited about it."

"My heart's there. My brain needs a little time to make the adjustment."

"I can live with that."

Chapter 29

Once again, the scaffolding was going up all over downtown in preparation for the annual Jack-O-Lantern Festival. The town was hoping to break their own Guinness World Record this year and Marybeth and Josh had done their part. Their carved pumpkins were sitting in the store window waiting for the sidewalk shelving to appear.

They were having their anniversary dinner at the Crabby Apple. The past week had been an emotional roller coaster for everyone and they were finally settling back down to what passed for normal.

"It seems that all's well that ends well." Josh raised his wine glass in a toast.

"Yes. Another caper backed by your mother completed." She clinked his glass. "I talked with my dad today and he says he's fine. Better than fine actually. He feels like a weight has been lifted."

"Just like the cards said," Josh reminded her.

"Oh, yeah. You're right. I hadn't thought of it since we pulled it last week."

"So, can we say that, even though my mother upsets the apple cart once in a while, it's all for the better?"

"Yes. I'll give it her. I just hope that next time she gives us a little more to go on and a little less pressure to get there."

"Oh, so you're already looking forward to next time?"

"No. I'd prefer there was never a next time, but I fear that your mother has carved a little niche for herself over there and we haven't heard the last of her."

Josh chuckled. "You're probably right. Do you think she can find me an apartment?"

"Funny you should say that. The apartment over the store just opened up."

"You're kidding?" Josh thought she was teasing him.

"Nope. The tenant is moving out December thirty-first."

Josh was grinning ear to ear. "Well, thanks Mom," he said looking up to the sky. He turned back to Marybeth. "What's it like up there?"

"It's actually quite nice, hard wood floors, lots of natural light, newly renovated."

"Would that make you crazy if I were upstairs?"

"No. Honestly, I'm getting used to the idea of you being around more. I'm looking forward to it."

"Great. I'll call the landlord before I leave."

They had said goodbye a dozen times over the past year but this time it seemed a little harder than before. "Yes, but that's not for a couple more days, so let's talk about something else."

"Okay you pick the topic."

"When are you starting your next book?"

"Oh my God! You're as bad as my mother!"

Epilogue

JAMES

After the intervention in the clearing, James was able to see hope again in his life. Sean's story helped him to understand that things can and will get better. Angie's story warned him that suicide is a tragedy that keeps on giving. He no longer considered it a viable option, no matter how bad things got. And there were some tough moments. Each trip to the counselor ripped off another emotional scab but also sent him home with less of a burden. So, he tolerated it as best he could. Eventually he ran out of scabs.

He met with Dean a few times and heard stories of his father and *their* war. He realized that they had more in common than he thought. Along with Ray, he coaxed Dean back into the society, proving that helping someone else helps yourself, too. They even went to the same AA meetings.

SEAN

Although out of sorts for a few weeks, Sean was able to get closure on a long-standing regret. The few symptoms he had of

PTSD remitted of their own accord. He was sleeping better than he ever had.

Initially he drove to Harrisburg once a week to accompany James to therapy, but it wasn't long before James was committed to the process and felt comfortable going on his own. Sean talked with him weekly and drove to Harrisburg as needed. He eventually told James the story of how he and Bobby met, and the strange yard sale that saved his life.

RAY

As Sean took over mentoring James, Ray helped Dean to access all the services available to vets. Substance abuse treatment resolved a lot of the issues initially. Then counseling for PTSD and medical attention cleaned up the rest. Social Security disability as well as military disability gave him enough income to be reasonably comfortable. Disabled American Vets, DAV, were great at finding him housing and setting him up with basic furnishings. Reconnecting to his family was a work in progress but their initial response was good.

Ray got the added bonus of Denise's company each time he visited the Vet Center, which made the drive from Pomroy well worth it.

JOSH

Josh, with Marybeth's help, settled in upstairs. He started his second novel for young adults and when he needed a break from writing, he went downstairs to see how he could be helpful. He eventually got involved with some of Marybeth's repurposing projects, adding some of his own handyman skills to the mix.

MARYBETH

Marybeth quickly got used to Josh being around. Even though he had an apartment, he was over her house often. And his willingness to assist with the shop reduced her overall stress. She began to let down her guard and imagine what the future might hold.

ANGIE

Angie and her mom had a long overdue conversation about Jackie's death. They both had come to terms with it in their own way, but sharing their grief reduced their pain and they began to replace it with happy stories and new memories.

Afterthoughts

SUICIDE

Suicide is always tragic. We've seen it, in recent years, in some of Hollywood's most beloved stars. It has lingering effects on those left behind, more so than any death we call *natural*.

According to the Center for Disease Control (CDC) suicide is the 10th leading cause of death in this country. These numbers do not consider deaths deemed accidental or undetermined, like single car accidents or accidental drug over-doses.

123 people per day complete a suicide.
3,000 souls attempt it.
An unknown number are hospitalized with intentions.

White males account for 70% of all completed suicides, most of them are fifty and older.

Suicide is the second leading cause of death in children 15 to 19, behind accidents, and the third leading cause of death in children 5 to 14, behind accidents and cancer.

Here is a link to statistics from Center for Disease Control National Center for Health Statistics: https://www.cdc.gov/nchs/fastats/child-health.htm

If you need help or want to help someone else, here's a good place to start.

National Suicide Prevention Hotline - Call 1-800-273-8255 https://suicidepreventionlifeline.org/

POST TRAUMATIC STRESS DISORDER (PTSD)

If you follow the news too closely, you can easily believe that our soldiers and veterans are all permanently broken. The fact is that only 11% of service members from the Middle East conflicts develop PTSD compared with 7.9% of the general population. More of a problem is the 22% who suffered a traumatic brain injury during the same conflicts.

Although PTSD won't usually go away on its own, it is completely treatable and curable. One of the difficulties in treating PTSD in veterans is the reluctance of vets to ask for help. Alcoholism and substance abuse often complicate treatment. Effective treatment starts with addressing addiction problems and resolving basic needs like housing and income.

http://www.ptsd.ne.gov/what-is-ptsd.html

Vet Centers have been set up in most cities and towns to assist our veterans with medical and mental health without having to drive hours to get to a VA hospital, but for many, the registration offices can be prohibitively far away. Disabled American Veterans, a charitable organization, is a great resource and will go the extra mile to assist all veterans and their families.

https://www.dav.org/

Although there is certainly a problem with identifying and treating our veterans, it is hopeful to note that the vast majority of veterans serve their tour of duty and return healthy, integrating back into civilian society without difficulty.

Author's Note

I am a veteran of the United States Air Force. I have spent many years working with active duty personnel and veterans to help them overcome service-related stress of all kinds. It is hoped that this story offers hope to old and new veterans alike and their families. Please reach out if you need help.

Please visit Marie's Website https://www.MLeClaire.com for more information, books and forums on topics she raises in her stories.

About the Author

Marie LeClaire has spent the past thirty years as a mental health counselor encouraging others to look beyond our sometimes-limited perspective and see a bigger picture of what influences our lives and guides our behavior. She has been writing novels and short stories for the past five years. She still does a little counseling part time, but her love now is purely fiction - sort of. After all, art imitates life, doesn't it? After wandering around much of her adult life, she currently calls Worcester, MA home.